JUNE FOSTER

The Inn at Cranberry Cove

June Foster

Copyright © 2020 by June Foster
Published by Forget Me Not Romances

This book is a work of fiction. Names, characters, places, and incidents are the product of the author's imagination and are used fictitiously. Any resemblance to actual events, locales, or persons, living or dead, is coincidental.

All rights reserved including the right to reproduce this book or portions thereof in any form whatsoever – except short passages for reviews – without express permission.

ISBN: 978-1-952661-43-3

Acknowledgements

I'd like to thank Kevin and Leanna Moos who provided the cover picture of their lovely boutique hotel in Ilwaco, Washington in which I set *The Inn at Cranberry Cove*. Years ago, my husband and I visited the inn on several occasions when we lived in Washington state so the B&B came to mind when I thought about where to set my story. The Inn at Harbor Village is a lovely facility which offers guests a unique experience surrounded by a woodland setting. I have fictionalized some of the features of the hotel. https://innatharbourvillage.com/

~~~~~~

I'd also like to express my deep gratitude and appreciation to Fay Lamb, my indispensable freelance editor who has to date edited every book I've ever written. Fay is an exceptional author of romantic suspense. *The Inn at Cranberry Cove* is one of my first attempts in this genre. Fay offered several plot changes which have greatly bettered the story.

Chapter One

Ashton Price took the keys offered by the executor of her aunt's will.

"As her attorney, I can tell you your aunt would be grateful if she knew you were perpetuating her life's dream. If only she could be here to witness the inn filled with visitors and bustling with activity once again."

Ashton sighed. She could barely believe that Aunt Gina would leave her entire life's work, her beautiful inn to Ashton's care. "After all she did for me…" Her memory meandered to the rebellious young Ashton of fifteen, and she cringed. "I've always wanted to be in business for myself."

He returned to the mahogany desk and handed her the box with Aunt Gina's jewelry. "She gave orders that I should present this to you upon her passing. She wanted me to advise you to put her valuables into safe keeping as soon as possible. She wanted me to expressly warn you that people have not forgotten the legend and to vet your visitors carefully. Some come looking for the treasure and snoop into places they shouldn't go."

Ashton smiled. Aunt Gina had often told her stories about the rumors. Early ancestors of the inn's previous owners had a cache of precious gems hidden in the home somewhere. She'd even allowed Ashton to search on her own. But Aunt Gina had assured her that it had only been a myth.

"I understand her reasoning, and that'll be the next order of business after I get settled." Ashton slipped the key in her purse and gripped the ornate wooden container. "I appreciate your work as her lawyer and hope I can depend on you as well."

"Of course. Gina always spoke of what a blessing you were to her."

"She changed my life. I'd probably be in prison today if it hadn't been for her."

Mr. Bradford stared at her. "What do you mean?"

"I'm surprised she didn't tell you. When I was a teen, my parents planned to send me to a girls' correctional ranch."

He frowned. "I can't imagine why."

"Let's just say I was a rebel and heading for a very unpleasant life until Aunt Gina stepped in. That's why I intend to keep her legacy."

Mr. Bradford smiled. "Well, in Gina's own words, you're an outstanding, college-educated young woman now." He looked at his watch. "My next client is waiting, but I wish you the best. I hope The Inn at Cranberry Cove prospers as it did when your aunt was alive."

Ashton shook the lawyer's hand. "I'm going to give it my best though no one can take Gina Price's place."

She walked out of the office, butterflies whirling in

her stomach. Life in Cranberry Cove would be nothing like it had been in the big city of Denver. Operating the inn was a challenge she'd never faced before. Even more challenging than her accounting job she'd left six weeks ago. But carrying Aunt Gina's legacy meant everything to her. If she failed, her aunt's dream would be lost forever.

James Atwood leaned over his desk at Pacific Cranberry, Incorporated. Nothing appeared to be amiss with the company's delivery schedule. Everything seemed to be working, but he couldn't dismiss the latest of several complaints of non-delivery and invoices received for items not obtained.

He scratched his head and then rubbed his eyes.

His office door opened. "It's after five, James." His secretary, Leslie Cunningham, followed her daily routine of checking to see if he needed one last thing before she left. "I'm good, Leslie. Thanks."

She smiled and started to close the door.

"Wait. Is Robert still in his office?"

Leslie's smirk told him all he needed to know. His cousin had probably left the office five minutes after returning from lunch. James would have to talk to him tomorrow. If they could remain in each other's company for more than five minutes, perhaps they'd be able to figure out the breakdown in the company's delivery system.

"See you in the morning." Leslie closed the door.

James turned off his computer, grabbed his keys

from the desk, and exited his office.

"Son." Dad stopped him in the hall. "Leaving so soon."

His father used the tired joke as a way to tell James he worked too hard. Dad had always been able to leave his job behind. Before, James hadn't been able to ... and he couldn't now after all that had happened.

James tried to make his smile genuine. He wasn't sure if he could succeed at that any longer. "Yeah. I figured I'd bug out a little early and get some gardening in."

Dad studied James for a long second. "I admire your work ethic, but you haven't stopped one minute since—"

James held up his hand, pleading silently for his father to drop what he was going to say. "I did stop, Dad. I stopped to sell the estate, to donate Bethany's clothes to charity, and to move ..." He swallowed the lump in his throat. "To move myself into the cabin. That was enough of a break, don't you think?"

Dad patted his shoulder. "Sometimes a man needs to stop in order to let his emotions catch up to him. If he doesn't, they may come out when he least expects it."

Dad didn't know, hadn't visited James when he was alone in the cabin, the door to one room closed, impossible for him to open because of the grief that was stored inside. That's why the gardening, away from home, the respite he'd been afforded meant so much to him. And he needed to get there ... and now. "You have a good evening, Dad. I'll see you in the morning."

The Inn at Cranberry Cove with its gray painted hardwood exterior and countless responsibilities loomed before Ashton. She pressed the brake. Perhaps she should turn and head back to Colorado. But, how could she? She shifted into drive and inched the car up in front of the inn. Aunt Gina had trusted her with her treasured possession. Didn't the wooden box on the passenger seat serve as a token of that faith? The air in her Jeep grew stale, and she opened the door for a long breath of the fragrant northwest air.

From his cage in back, Maxwell meowed a long, pleading appeal.

"It's okay, buddy. I'll get you in a moment. Be patient."

Ashton stepped out of the car. Nothing had changed since her last visit. Nothing, that is, but her place of employment.

The inn belonged to her now, though if she could choose, she'd rather have Aunt Gina alive and on this earth.

She locked the car and trekked around the east side of the building that once served as a chapel.

The gardens with the birdbath, the fountain, and the tiered landscaping were well-kept as if someone tended them, though the inn was empty.

The stone path led past the wooden deck with the wicker lawn chairs. Only a year ago visitors had enjoyed the afternoon sun while drinking icy lemonade and munching cranberry scones.

Ashton meandered past the Japanese snowbell tree and the fragrant honeysuckle, bringing back memories of visits to Cranberry Cove.

The elm Ashton used to climb appeared ahead. It cast dark shadows on the gravestone.

She steadied herself, gripping the tree's trunk. The stone marker where Aunt Gina's ashes were buried stood beneath its shade. Her soul was absent from the earth and no doubt present with her Lord.

Ashton wiped a tear and knelt. She drew her fingers along the curve of the rough rock. *Virginia Price. Here lies the ashes of the beloved daughter, sister, and aunt. John 3:16.* Then the dates she was born and died.

But *wife and mother* were absent from the inscription. Why hadn't her aunt married? Ashton would never be able to ask her now.

Aunt Gina's workshop—actually a small wooden building with glass windows whose clarity had been lessened by moisture stood a few yards from the gravesite. Ashton pushed the door open and stepped inside. The walls were in need of a good cleaning. Pieces her aunt had finished prior to her death filled the area. Aunt Gina had thrown herself into her art. She loved her intricate work of stained-glass, and her creative streak had earned her a place among the best of the craft.

One of Ashton's goals was to preserve that work and make it an added attraction for the inn. She walked out the door and returned to the gravesite again.

A sturdy metal vase with fresh yellow roses sat next to the marker for her aunt's resting place. They couldn't possibly be left from the funeral she'd attended thirty days ago. Someone had obviously been here recently to pay Aunt Gina's grave a visit. But who?

Inside the inn, she explored the first floor, the

décor and furniture the same as she remembered as a teen. At the entrance to the inn, the majestic staircase took her breath away.

Up the stairs at the landing leading to the second floor, something looked different. A lovely stained-glass window had replaced the old one from before. If only she could ask her aunt about the beautiful design in the glass, but it was too late.

JUNE FOSTER

Chapter Two

Ashton had rambled around the home most of the day, looking into rooms, taking inventory, and re-familiarizing herself with the layout. Aunt Gina had lived in an apartment attached to the inn and accessible through the inside, so Ashton had unpacked her clothes—and Maxwell—in there before exploring.

She stepped to the landing to examine the exquisite stained-glass window her aunt had created and installed, but a noise from the backyard drew her attention.

Ashton hurried down the stairs and into the kitchen. June air flowed through the open window, hinting of the lilies and hydrangeas now in bloom out back. The continued sound of scraping like a shovel on gravel called her outside.

A man in jeans and a plaid shirt that swallowed his frame bent over as he made long swipes with a rake, collected leaves, twigs, and sticks. He gathered the debris into a pile and lifted the rubble into a wheelbarrow. But why was he working in the yard?

She took the steps down onto the lawn. "Excuse me."

The man pivoted toward her. "Oh, hello. I saw your car, but I didn't want to disturb you. You're Ashton. We met at the funeral, but it was a brief hello. Before she passed, Gina told me she had faith you'd come." He dropped the rake, wiped his palms down his jeans, and offered his hand. "I'm James Atwood."

Ashton narrowed her eyes. This man in his early thirties with soft blue eyes, and a seeming trustworthy demeanor said all the right things, but why would he be in the backyard of the inn this late in the evening. "Yes, I'm Ashton Price. What are you doing here?"

The man lowered his hand. "I kept the garden for Gina before she passed and helped her with odd jobs." He rubbed the back of his neck. "I hope you don't mind if I continue to look after the yard. I don't want her lawn to go to seed or the flowers to die."

That sounded likely, but could he be lying to her, thinking he would look for the legendary gems? He could say anything he wanted about Gina. She wasn't here to confirm or deny. "Thank you, but I'm afraid I can't afford a gardener right now."

"That's not a problem. Gina paid me for the rest of the year."

Ashton frowned. "I'll have to check my ledgers for the expense."

"I understand." He smiled. "Your aunt was like a second mother to me. She befriended me and saw me through…" He cleared his throat and picked up the rake again. "I mean… she was easy to talk to, and we became friends. It's the least I can do. Her garden is important to me." James turned back to his work again, raking the rubbish into another pile.

Before doing anything else, she needed to discover

whether James Atwood spoke the truth. She took the stairs to the deck again. If she found no record of payment, her next course of action would be to call 9-1-1.

James finished raking the section of the yard closest to the deck and replaced the tool in the shed. His next project—the fountain. He removed the pump and drained the water from the bowl-shaped top.

Scrubbing the pump and fountain was a distraction, something to tire him out and allow him to fall asleep without regrets keeping him awake.

Thoughts of Gina reminded him why he had taken on the job, and those thoughts would lead him to places he didn't want to go. He shook off the memories and headed to the tool shed for his scrub brush and cleaning solution.

It was almost eerie how much Gina's niece looked like her. If he knew anything about women, Ms. Price didn't trust him. But he wanted to continue working among the blooms, the tall elms, and the fescue grass. He wasn't ready to go back to his old life—at least for a few more weeks.

At the built-in desk in the kitchen, Ashton closed her aunt's ledger. As the gardener had said, Aunt Gina had paid him a lump sum for the rest of the year, though she was sure the able-bodied man could make three times as much working somewhere else.

If Gina trusted him to take care of her yard, it would likely be safe for Ashton to allow him to continue working. She had to admit that she needed his help. She couldn't run the inn and keep the yard up. Still, she couldn't be too careful.

Ashton walked to the window and peered out.

James stood by the fountain scrubbing the bowl with more vigor than she'd probably muster. What was it about him? Although dressed in work clothes, his eyes, the way he held his shoulders gave him a look of sophistication. Somehow, she didn't believe he'd always worked as a gardener.

Back at the desk, she perused the ledger then the computer. Her sweet aunt hadn't attempted a spreadsheet. Given Ashton's experience as an accountant for the last eight years, setting up the B&B on a software program would be no problem.

By seven, Ashton figured she'd done enough for one day.

She peeked out the window for the tenth time, curious as to when James would go home. The shadows out back grew longer, and the sun would set in another hour.

A newer Lexus was parked by the road on the east side of the inn. She hadn't noticed it before, and she doubted a gardener could afford to drive that model.

Could someone be prowling around out there? But a burglar wouldn't stalk the area in daylight. Maybe having James around was a good idea. Though she wondered how well he'd fare against an intruder. Didn't he have a wife to feed him?

A man walked toward the Lexus and got in. When he turned to back out, she saw his face. James.

Ashton wrinkled her brow. How could a gardener afford a luxury car? Surely, he hadn't stolen it? No. Gina would never have hired a thief. And knowing her aunt, she'd struck up conversations with the man and knew his life story after the first week.

Maxwell curled around her ankle and meowed.

"I know. You're ready for dinner. Let's go to the apartment." She locked the kitchen door that led to the outside, turned off the lights, and headed down the hall to the living quarters Aunt Gina had previously occupied.

Maxwell's meows accompanied her all the way.

"Okay, I get the message. You're starved. You didn't eat a sandwich like I did a while ago."

After he finished his kitty chow, Maxwell curled up in his cozy fleece bed and closed his eyes.

"Good idea, buddy. I'm tired too from my hard work today."

After a soak in Gina's classic porcelain enamel tub, she dried off with one of the oversized, white towels.

Lace doilies covered the top of the old-fashioned mahogany vanity. She opened the empty drawers on the left where Aunt Gina had kept makeup and brushes.

The bottom one remained locked, but she remembered the little key on the keychain with the housekeys. The attorney had given them to her on the day of her aunt's funeral. She pulled it out of her purse and opened the vanity with a click then reached in. Nothing. She extended her arm farther and grasped a small book.

Leather straps wrapped around the dark brown

leather journal. Aunt Gina's.

The duvet covers invited her to relax. She undid the journal's straps, heart pounding. The distinctive handwriting was the same as on the letters Aunt Gina had written through the years with words of encouragement. She opened to a page toward the end dated April 1 of this year.

Today Lidia Mason called from Oceanview. Her husband can install my stained-glass window in a few days. I can't wait to enjoy it. This one, I made for myself, to commemorate the greatest love and loss of my life. It's visible from the entrance as well as on the stairs to the second floor.

Ashton flipped to the next page dated April 17 of this year.

I'm grateful to have James taking care of the grounds. He drives to the inn every day from his little cabin down the road, ready to work. He's honest and always does more than I ask. I can't afford to pay him much.

Well, it looked like Ashton could trust James. After she read a few more lines, her eyelids grew heavy.

She must have drifted off, but a noise brought Ashton fully awake. What time was it? She glanced at her cell phone on the bedtable. One in the morning.

Were the sounds from within the inn? Had Maxwell gotten out of the room, though she thought she'd closed her apartment door.

She reached for the flashlight she'd stowed on the side table.

Maxwell was curled up at the end of the bed like he did most nights.

Maybe she'd dreamed the sound, or the house had

creaked. She held her breath and listened. Nothing.

Lying in bed again, she pulled the covers to her shoulders. "It's going to take a while to get used to this old building. Right, Maxwell?"

JUNE FOSTER

Chapter Three

James rapped on the door to the office next to his. He waited.

Leslie, in her cubicle outside his office, stood and shook her head.

What made James think Robert would arrive at work on time? The clock meant something to Uncle Terrance and to Dad. James had always been punctual despite the fact the workday clock meant nothing to him—that is, until he had another job, one that brought him the peace he needed.

Pacific Cranberry was a family-owned business, and though James tended to work hard, mainly because he avoided going home, things moved smoothly except where his cousin, Robert, was involved. People said at first glance they could be mistaken for twins. Once people got to know either of them, James prayed they were never confused.

"You looking for me?"

The question came without warning and startled James.

Robert stood as close to James as one could get—a territorial issue, James was sure. "Yeah. Got a minute?"

Robert shrugged and opened his door, letting it fall open and leaving James to follow.

James stood in front of Robert's desk. Ludicrous. The Vice President of Marketing for one of the best-known cranberry operations in the State of Washington should not have to probe for answers from the Vice President of Distribution, namely Robert.

James took a deep breath and let it out.

"Well?" Robert kicked out his chair and sat down, hands raised. "Spill it out, Golden Boy. You only seek me out when there's a problem."

True enough. They'd never gotten along. James didn't understand why, but even as children, they were always ready to pick a fight. Throughout their school years, they avoided each other. At the job, if they recognized the other in passing, that was a good day. "I've been receiving some calls from customers. I'm trying to plug up some holes in a sinking ship, but we're about to lose accounts."

"What's that got to do with me?" Robert leaned back, his hands behind his head.

"Distribution, Robert. That's what it's about. I'm out there making contacts, getting the sales, and when I follow up, I'm told that deliveries haven't been made but like clockwork, invoices arrive."

"Check with Leslie. She's our secretary."

James stood silent for a long moment, weighing his next words. "She's my secretary. You can't keep one long enough to learn the job so Leslie has to do it. She's efficient, and I've never had a problem with her. You handle distribution, so you need to get on the line to the warehouse and find out what's going on."

Robert leaned forward. "You do your job. I'll do

mine, and if Leslie has a problem with doing my work, she can tell me."

Something the single mother would never do. Robert had a way of twisting the truth, and sometimes Dad sided with Uncle Terrance and Robert in order to avoid a family conflict.

"How's that cabin working out for you?" Robert asked.

James wasn't aware Robert knew he'd sold the estate and moved. "It suits."

"It suits," Robert mimicked. "You had it all: that big house, a beautiful wife, a son. And you threw it all away. Maybe that's the way you always wanted it."

James fisted his hand on the top of Robert's desk. His cousin had hit a soft target. Maybe James hadn't wanted all he had, but he would never have wanted to lose what he lost in the way he had lost it. "I'll e-mail you the names of the businesses missing deliveries and receiving invoices. I want a report on my desk detailing what you discovered before you leave the building today."

James slammed Robert's door on his way out.

Leslie stood once again, but James waved her off and went into his office.

This time, he shut the door a little more softly, but he wished with all his might that he could have shut it hard enough to break out the windows.

Sometimes, all he wanted to do was to strangle his cousin.

But that would be just another death he'd have to live with.

Ashton ventured into the old shed looking for some tools. She had a picture she wanted to hang in her apartment as well as a small stained-glass piece that when placed above the window would catch the sun's rays and bring color into the room.

She stumbled over an old wooden stand and opened up a cabinet door.

The shed's lightbulb needed more wattage. She could barely see anything inside. Why hadn't she brought a flashlight with her?

A scuffling sounded outside.

Ashton turned.

The door slammed with a bang, jolting her.

Her hand to her throat, she took a deep breath. The windows were dirty, but she could see the plants outside. There hadn't been a breeze strong enough to cause the door to close that hard.

She ventured forward and turned the knob.

It didn't budge. She pushed against the door. "Hello. Hello. Is someone out there?"

She held her breath and listened.

A shadow fell over her, and she spun around. Had someone been looking in the window from the outside? There was no one there now.

"Hello." She tried the knob again.

The bolt lock was on the outside, and she'd used the key the lawyer gave her.

She patted her pockets. No cell phone and no key. She slumped forward. She must have left the key in the lock.

Had the wind closed it so soundly that it had turned the lock?

She tried the window. It was bolted shut.

Today was Saturday. James Atwood had graced her with his presence every afternoon. She had no reason to suspect that he'd give up his Saturday to work around the yard. Aunt Gina hadn't paid him enough for that.

In case the third time would be a charm, she tried the door again.

Then she slid down to the dirty wooden flooring. She could be in here until Monday afternoon unless someone happened by.

James planted his feet on the dirt walkway and pivoted toward the old log building where he'd lived for the last six weeks. Before he rented the cabin, his life had limped along, submerged in a failing marriage. Then, without warning, nothing was the same.

He crawled into his car and rubbed his tired eyes. The big house on the hill intruded upon his memory. If he never saw it again, it'd be okay. Everything he wanted out of the estate was inside the cabin, and the new owners had seemed a very happy family. He winced. The thought drove a knife to his gut.

He gunned the motor, turning out onto the main road to his job at the inn.

The beauty of the tree-lined road and the Saturday morning dew reflecting golden sparkles of light reminding him of Gina's vibrant personality. Calmer now, he took a breath. She'd helped him believe that in adversity we grow. As Isaiah from the Bible said, we only need to take His right hand and not be afraid because God will help us.

He stopped beside the inn in his usual spot. Each day, the allure of Gina's garden—the flowering plants, the coastal air—reminded him that God offered forgiveness, that He would restore his life in time. He set out for the tool shed to get his work gloves and the hoe. Those weeds would be more plentiful than the flowers if he didn't get rid of them.

He made it halfway to the shed but stopped. Ashton had met him each evening when he arrived, and they'd had a brief conversation. Maybe he should announce his morning arrival. She might not be expecting him.

He passed the fountain and crossed the lawn until he reached the path leading to the deck. He walked up the steps and tapped on the door.

To his right, muddy footprints he hadn't noticed before trailed from the edge of the porch to the back door. No doubt Ashton had come out earlier. Stood to reason. The property belonged to her, after all.

After a moment, he knocked again.

Strange. Her car was parked out front. Maybe she was cleaning and didn't hear him. He shrugged and headed toward the shed.

He slipped his key inside the bolt lock, and but it didn't turn to unlock. Instead, it locked.

"Hello," a muffled voice called. "Is someone out there? I'm locked inside."

James shook his head and unlocked the door, swinging it wide open.

"Oh, thank goodness. I wondered if you worked weekends." Ashton got to her feet.

"What are you doing?" He laughed.

She scowled in his direction. "I was looking for a hammer and nails," she huffed. "The door slammed shut, and I guess my key was in the lock, and it must have been hard enough to turn it."

James held up his own key. "These are mine. I used them, but the door wasn't locked."

Ashton patted her shorts pocket and raised her hands as if to ask a question. "I'm telling you I couldn't get the knob to turn."

"Step out for a minute," he directed.

She did as he asked.

He closed the door and turned the knob. The door opened easily. "Ashton, I put the key in the lock, and when I turned it, I locked it. You were not locked in."

"Oh, for goodness' sake." She stalked into the shed and over to the work counter. There, she picked up her keys and stared at them as if she couldn't believe they were real. "I'm working to get things in order. Maybe I've done too much."

The creases that occurred with the furrow of her brow showed her confusion. He needed to change the course of her day. "Let's pretend it didn't happen. Good morning."

She blinked. "Good morning."

"I was going to ask if you were the culprit that left the muddy footprints. I guess I have my answer."

"I haven't muddied up anything. I came outside to the shed, got locked—or shut—inside, and haven't been back."

Well, he'd brought that conversation right back to

where they'd started and not where he wanted to be.

Ashton trekked onto the deck, her slender frame in white shorts and a pink sweater. She glanced at the muddy prints, a frown on her face. "After the shed incident, I don't expect you to believe me, but I haven't been near this area." She rubbed her forehead. "I... last night I thought I heard something."

James faced her. "What?"

"A noise. The sound woke me, but I can't be sure. I might've imagined that as well."

He hated to scare her, but he wanted to help. "About what time?"

"I looked at my phone. Around one."

"Listen. If you hear any more sounds in the night, call me—as well as the police. I'll be happy to come over and check around outside." He extended his hand. "Let me see your phone, and I'll add my number to your contacts." He swallowed his nervous chuckle.

"I left it inside." Ashton stepped into the kitchen, retrieved her cell phone from the table, and handed it to him. "Do you have a family at home? I wouldn't want to disturb anyone."

"No. I don't have anyone at home." People usually didn't ask the question. Most in Cranberry Cove knew his story.

She reached for her cell after he put in his number. "Thank you. I hope there's no need. Just a second." She returned to the kitchen and then stepped out onto the deck, passing him a business card. "You're the first to get one of these."

James stuffed the card in his jeans pocket. "Maybe it would be wise to take some security measures such as electronic door locks."

"It sounds like a good idea, but I'll have to wait until I start making a profit."

James studied Ashton's face. Her eyes, the color of a field of clover, fascinated him. Determination and self-confidence radiated from her face. "Your aunt and I became friends." He pointed to the wooden lawn chair. "We'd talk for an hour sometimes. Her faith in God was so evident. Even when she found out she had breast cancer. It didn't get her down. She told me she'd see the Lord that much sooner."

Ashton peered at him. "She once shared the Lord with me, too. It changed my life. But I haven't been to church since…"

He waited for her to say more. Obviously, she didn't want to talk about something. "I used to shy away from God, too. But Gina explained how we can't blame Him for adversity. Adversity deepens our relationship with Him." Yet why should he lecture her? He didn't blame God for what happened. He was too ashamed to attend church—didn't know how to give God the guilt that had eaten his insides for the last two months.

He brushed a hand through his hair. Tough subject. Let it drop for now. "I figure Gina was your father's sister since you both have the same last name."

"Yes. He and my mom travel in their RV. They're in Denver right now. I'm hoping they'll come to Washington to visit some time."

He shifted from one foot to the other. "Denver's a beautiful part of the country. It must've been fun growing up in the area."

She nodded. "What about you? Are you from here?"

"Yes, I am." He needed to back out of this

conversation as well.

"Yoo-hoo. Hello."

James smiled. Mrs. Babbage to the rescue. "Have you met Edith Babbage yet?"

"No." Ashton waved toward the older woman who stood at the fence separating the properties.

"Edith and Gina were unlikely friends. Gina admitted that the Lord must have placed Edith in her life to teach her patience. You should say hello, but if there's anything you don't want others to know, don't tell her."

"Thanks for the info." Ashton smiled and headed to meet Mrs. Babbage.

James breathed a sigh of relief. There were certainly things he didn't want Ashton Price to know right now.

Chapter Four

Ashton had enjoyed her chat with Mrs. Babbage on Saturday. Though the older woman had fished for information, Ashton had managed to shy away from the bait and the hook. What she had intended as a quick conversation ended an hour later with Mrs. Babbage's teary-eyed promise to deliver a dessert to welcome Gina's niece to her new home.

They'd spent Sunday afternoon having tea and eating a delicious crumb cake. Mrs. Babbage had informed Ashton that she provided desserts for the inn because it gave her something to do, and that a Mrs. Mayberry had worked for Aunt Gina, taking a large burden from her and allowing Gina to work on her art and to run that part of the businesses that kept the bills paid.

The time with Mrs. Babbage had been relaxing, but both Saturday night and Sunday night had Ashton tossing and turning. The noise, the muddy footprints, the incident with the shed, Ashton was either worn out and imagining things or something was going on. Of course, Edith Babbage's claims of ghostly lights in the home since Gina's death were enough to add to the worries that haunted Ashton at night.

Now, Ashton lifted the box with Aunt Gina's jewelry from the top shelf in her closet and grabbed her keys.

In his kitty bed, Maxwell stretched his legs and meowed.

"Hey, buddy. I wonder if someone knew about the broaches and bracelets and tried to steal them the other night or locked me in the shed so they could look in the day. Maybe James's arrival foiled their attempt. What do you think? Or have I developed an overactive imagination? There were footprints on the deck, you know."

Maxwell yawned and curled up on the bed again.

"I'm sure you agree." She eyed her cat.

His closed eyes clued her in. He wasn't worried about the jewelry.

In Cranberry Cove, she turned left on Main toward the bank. If anyone was after Aunt Gina's possessions, they'd give up as soon as they learned the jewelry was in safe keeping.

Pacific Cranberry, Inc., stood on the same spot she remembered—the company that had grown along with the town and helped Cranberry Cove thrive. None of Cranberry Cove's buildings seemed to have changed since her childhood. The town still gave the impression of a frontier settlement.

At the end of the block, Ashton parked behind the bank. For the last time, she opened the box. "I promise to keep this safe for you, Aunt Gina," she whispered.

She ran her fingers down each side of the precious possession her aunt once cherished. On the right, she felt a little ridge, one she hadn't noticed before. She pushed on the smooth surface and a small drawer popped open. She giggled. A secret compartment.

Inside, a tiny velvet bag was tucked away. How had she missed this? She poked her finger in and withdrew something solid—a charm—one Aunt Gina apparently hadn't attached to her bracelet.

She turned the gold heart over and read the words inscribed on the back. *I'll always love you. R.J.*

Ashton's pulse throbbed in her throat. So, Aunt Gina once had a suitor. But who? She'd never know now, but the thought delighted her. "You weren't always alone. You had a secret love." She returned the charm to the bag and headed into the bank.

An hour later, she was an official resident of Cranberry Cove, if having a bank account meant anything. She tucked the key to the safety deposit box in her purse. Her next chore—buying groceries.

In front of Hometown Market, she drew the list from her pocket.

The morning sun shone through her windshield, warming her face. What was it about Cranberry Cove? She loved the small town that lacked the traffic and bustle of Denver. She breathed a long, relaxing sigh. Had God sent her here? Why would He? She hadn't spoken to Him since she'd gotten fired from her job.

She shook off the thoughts, grabbed a basket, then walked in through the opening of the sliding glass door. In produce, she selected a carton of bright red strawberries and a bag of ripe peaches. When guests started to arrive, strawberry-peach coffee cake would be at the top of her breakfast menu. Mrs. Babbage had asked if she could continue providing desserts, but Ashton wanted to do some of the cooking as well.

Guests. She bit the inside of her cheek. Was she really capable of running the inn with as much success as Aunt Gina? Given the potential for break-ins or illegal entries, she needed to start by making sure no others had a key in their possession. Or she'd have to change the locks.

Ashton stored the last of the refrigerated items in the fridge and stacked the can goods in the pantry.

From the window, she peered at James. As usual, he'd arrived after five.

He stood next to the honeysuckle holding the hose at the base of the plant. The water slowly dripped onto the soil. If she were to guess, his mind was on something besides watering. But what?

She swallowed hard and walked out on the deck. She had to ask the question even if it made him believe she suspected him of entering the inn the other night.

James looked up. "Hey."

"Morning." Ashton walked nearer. "Did my aunt provide you with any other keys?"

He stared a moment then dug in his pocket. "I have keys to all the buildings. She gave them to me when I became the gardener and unofficial handyman for the inn." He held out his hand showing her a keychain with a little cross and several keys attached. "Would you like them back?"

Now she felt stupid. If Aunt Gina had given him access to the entire place, she'd obviously trusted him. She'd said as much in her journal entry. "No, I just need to keep track of where they are. I'm sure I'll need repairs done, too."

James turned off the water at the spigot. "Ashton, you may have doubts about me, and I wouldn't blame you. But I can assure you, I cared deeply for your aunt and would do nothing to harm anyone she loved." He scratched the back of his neck. "I love the Lord as well and don't want to disobey Him."

His eyes twinkled when he said the words. Unless he'd taken acting lessons, he meant what he said.

JUNE FOSTER

Chapter Five

Ashton sat at her kitchen table alone and eating a sandwich she'd made while the canned soup she'd cooked cooled.

James had departed, as usual, after dark had fallen. She really did need to repay him with a meal or something. Gina had not paid the man enough for the work he did.

A car door closing caught her attention.

Even Maxwell stretched and came to full attention at her feet.

Ashton slipped out of the kitchen and eased down the hall.

A knock sounded as she reached the front door.

She jumped. "Yes?" she called from behind the locked door.

"Hello. Ms. Price. Uh ... Gina ... it's the Claxtons. We've arrived," a woman announced.

Claxtons. Claxtons.

"I'm sorry, but Gina is no longer here. I'm not familiar with your name." Ashton placed her hand on the door, wary of opening it to strangers.

"Now, that can't be," a man said. "We paid good

money to Gina Price. We have an extended reservation here, and it's been a long drive. Are you telling me the woman closed up shop and didn't let us know?"

Guests? Ashton wasn't ready for guests, but if she turned them away, the power of negative reviews could kill her business before she reopened.

She turned the knob. "Please come in. Please. I need to explain to you …"

"Explain?" The woman standing on the front porch drooped forward. "It's a long drive from California. We're bone tired, honey. If you tell us we booked a room for three months, and we can't stay here, I'm going to burst out in tears." She swiped at the blonde hair, heavy with hairspray and stepped out of her high heels. "Have a little mercy on us, will you?"

Ashton ushered them inside. "Please come in. Have a seat." She showed them into the living room.

"Oh, it's as charming as I remember it, Oggie." The woman twirled as if enchanted by her surroundings.

Oggie, though, wore a frown. "Ma'am, would you tell us what's going on?"

Again, Ashton motioned for them to take a seat. When they sat in the love seat, she took the chair across from them. "You see, I'm Ashton Price. Gina was my aunt—"

"Was? Oh, my. That means—" The woman gasped. "Oh, honey, I'm so sorry."

"Thank you."

"And you're here to close an estate or something?" Oggie's demeanor went neutral. "The inn's closed?"

"No. I actually plan to reopen. It's just that I thought Gina had canceled all the reservations. I haven't started accepting them until I familiarize myself with a new type of business. I don't recall seeing your name when I checked to assure Aunt Gina had been able to reach all of her guests."

"Well, of course, you don't, or we wouldn't be here, young lady."

"Now, Oggie, she's lost her aunt. She can't be expected to handle everything perfectly." The woman stood halfway and reached out a well-manicured hand. "I'm Beatrice, and this is my husband, Oggie. We were here a long time ago before the house became an inn. When we decided we wanted to return for a visit, we found an advertisement, and we set the reservation over a year ago. Oggie just retired, and we wanted to get right to enjoying life. We decided upon an extended stay here, and we paid in full. I can't imagine …"

Ashton pushed her lips into a smile. That had been about the time Aunt Gina was taking treatments, and as Ashton had learned from Mrs. Babbage, Gina was the reservation taker. Aunt Gina spoke with every would-be guest. Ashton supposed she'd allowed this reservation to slip through the cracks. But Ashton would've remembered their name if she'd run across a reservation not yet cancelled.

Oggie's face softened. "I can see we hit a nerve, little lady. I can admit that you aren't responsible for this, but is it possible for us to work this out. Beatrice has been so excited about staying here. What if we take room and not board? Just a place to stay and relax while we're out and about? We'll call it even. You shouldn't have to pay in full for your aunt's mistake, and we'll make do."

"I couldn't ask you to pay for a full reservation and not receive the full benefit." Ashton took a deep breath.

"I admit this has caught me off guard, but if you're willing to be patient, I'd like to welcome you to The Inn at Cranberry Cove."

Beatrice clapped her hands, and Oggie stood. He held out his hand to Ashton. "Thank you, pretty lady."

The man sure had a lot of adjectives that went in front of *lady*, but if it kept Ashton from a bad review, she'd let him call her anything. "If you want to bring in your luggage, I'll prepare the paperwork for sign-in, and once we have that completed, if you'll give me ten minutes to make sure your room is ready, we'll get you settled in. And for how long did you say you'd reserved a room?"

Oggie looked at Beatrice and then tugged her to his side. "Three months for my sweetie."

"I'll need the departure date."

Beatrice bit a nail. "I set the reservation for exactly ninety days." She followed Oggie to the door.

With a half-smile and half-grimace, Ashton made her way to the computer where she counted out ninety days, entered the reservation, and printed the paperwork needed.

She'd hoped for a little rest tonight, but with strangers inside the inn, and her aunt's admonition ringing in her brain, she'd probably need to sleep with one eye open for a few nights, at least.

Chapter Six

At the kitchen desk, Ashton leaned against the back of her chair and lifted her chin. One week at the inn and she'd transferred the ledger data to the computer with the program that made running the B&B simpler. The finances, breakfast menus, reservations, even keeping track of cleaning guest rooms was available at a touch of the mouse or cell phone. Of course, her one reservation had been unplanned and missing altogether from the data, but maybe the Claxtons' arrival had been a good thing. Rather than several guests at once, she could practice on the couple. They'd been very agreeable, and except for breakfast, they were enjoying eating out at places in and around the area. She rarely saw them except for a brief time in the morning.

She rose from the desk and stretched her arms above her. It had felt good to get a full night's sleep last night. No more strange sounds since the day after she'd arrived, and having someone else in the inn with her after the first night or two had settled her nerves. As she'd thought—the century old inn possessed its share of bumps and creaks, and she needed to get used to the noises. She'd obviously been mistaken about that first night. Being alone, she had imagined the worst. And the footprints and the incident with the shed she chalked up to her forgetfulness and clumsiness due to fatigue.

Earlier, the Claxtons had been eating breakfast with her. Beatrice had received a text and jumped up suddenly. "Oggie, our appointment!" she exclaimed, and they'd clamored upstairs and called a good-bye soon after.

Ashton laughed. They were a cute, but odd, couple.

She downed the last of the coffee in her mug. One more cup to see her through the rest of the morning.

She grasped the pot's handle then stopped. The carafe was empty, and she went to the sink to refill it. The water slowly dripped from the faucet. It needed a new washer, but plumbing repairs weren't her area of expertise.

James.

Should she ask him? Unless she wanted to pay a plumber to come out, it might be a good idea.

After she brewed the coffee, she filled her cup and glanced through the window. Strange, but James stood outside on a weekday morning. Usually, he arrived shortly after 5:00 p.m.

He whipped off his cap, wiped his brow, and plopped it back on his head. Then, he heaved the shovel into the earth, loosening the dirt under the ash tree near the deck. A variety of annuals in pots sat a few feet away, no doubt waiting to be planted.

Ashton took a second cup from the cabinet. Only fair to share with the hardworking guy. From the foil-wrapped covered pan, she sliced a generous piece of cinnamon coffee cake, grabbed a napkin, and took the mini-breakfast outside.

"Good morning." She set everything on the end table.

James glanced up from the ash tree.

"I thought you might like some coffee and breakfast cake I baked."

His eyes widened. Then he wiped his brow, leaving a dirty smear on his forehead. "Thanks. I hope you don't mind my being here on a weekday morning. I needed a change of pace. I was getting ready to trim the hedges in front next. Then I remembered your guests, but I didn't see a car. Still, I wanted to do something a little quieter until you said it was okay."

"They left earlier than usual, and you deserve a break, even a morning one. I'll just leave everything here." She set the cup and plate on a side table. "Would you be able to fix a leak on the kitchen sink faucet?"

"Sure. What's the problem?"

"I've got the faucet turned off, but the water keeps dripping."

He removed the gloves and poked them in his pocket. "I have some extra parts in the tool shed."

"Better you venture in there than me." Ashton chuckled. "I'd appreciate it." The bed on the side of the yard bloomed with summer flowers. "Look, I know those plants aren't free. Give me a receipt, and I'll pay you for them."

He smiled. "No. That's not necessary. I've still got money left from the funds Gina provided for yard supplies." He rinsed his hands under the outside water faucet. "I'll grab the coffee while it's still hot." He walked to the deck and sat in a chair near the table.

What would it hurt to chat with him a moment before she went to clean the Claxtons' room? Maybe she'd discover a little of what dwelled behind his quiet, guarded nature. She pulled up a chair near his and glanced toward the side yard. "Do you have a long drive to the inn?"

"No. I live in a small cottage a couple of miles south of here." He took a bite of coffee cake and wiped his mouth with the napkin. "I'll get on that faucet job this afternoon."

But was it right to ask him to do so much on the small salary Gina had already paid him? "I really want to be fair about how much you make at the inn. I'm sure you could get more somewhere else. And I know what it feels like to worry about finances." But he wouldn't be interested in her employment failures.

"Problems in a former job?"

By the look on his face, he sincerely wanted to know. "Yeah. One of the reasons I left." She lifted her hand in a stop position. "You probably think I ran away from my problems. More than anything, I came here for Aunt Gina."

"I can understand that. What happened?"

Ashton gazed at the gardens awakening with color. Sharing her past with James—maybe it was a good thing—as if the mere act of telling another would lighten the load.

James's peered at her with those soft blue eyes, waiting.

"I—" The words got stuck on her tongue. She swallowed.

He sat forward and set his coffee cup on the table. "Ashton…?"

She took a quick breath. "I worked for an accounting firm in Denver. My boss became my boyfriend, though looking back, that wasn't wise."

"Did you break it off?" He took a healthy bite of the coffee cake and chewed.

"Yes, but only after an incident occurred."

James leaned back in his seat never taking his attention off her.

She began the story. She'd better finish. "There was a co-worker who wanted my job—and my boyfriend."

He frowned.

"Some of the paperwork my clients provided went missing, delaying completion of the accounts. The clients complained to Rick, my boss and boyfriend. Later the documents showed up on my desk."

James crossed his arms over his chest.

"After a few weeks, the same thing happened again. Rick didn't believe me when I said I had no idea how it happened. We began seeing each other less outside of the office. Then one day, he called me in. He said several of the women employees complained about my work ethic, said I wasn't doing my job."

"That doesn't seem like the Ashton who's determined to run her aunt's business."

"I worked hard for that company."

James shook his head and sat back in the chair.

"Rick said he thought I was taking advantage of our relationship. That my work was getting sloppy." Again, the jabs of humiliation stung.

"How did you find out who complained?"

"I demanded Rick tell me. He said no and that he had to let me go." Ashton picked at a thread on her jeans. "After it was over, Rick discovered the other accountant had enlisted the secretary to back up her lies. She'd nabbed the files when I went to lunch and hid them. I was stupid to leave them out in the first place." Ashton gripped her fist into a ball. "Rick fired the other two and wanted to hire me again, but I said no. The part that hurt the most was he'd believed them over me. He worked long hours, and just to be with him, I had worked, too. For him to believe them over me was like a slap in the face."

"I'm sorry. That must've been tough."

"Yes, but right after my firing, I got the letter from the lawyer about the completion of my aunt's estate and that the inn was ready for me to claim. With all my heart, I wanted to carry on my aunt's legacy." She gazed at the Douglas fir to the back of the property. "I didn't mean to tell you my life story. I'd like to hear more about you. You said Gina helped you through a tough time."

He shifted in the chair then rubbed his neck. "I—"

A honeybee hovered not more than a foot in front of Ashton. She yelped and sprinted toward the backdoor, fanning her face. "Oh, I hate those things."

James stood. "They generally don't bite unless they feel threatened."

She raised her right hand. "I promise, Mr. Bee, I won't bother you."

He chuckled. "Gotta get to work." He took the steps to the lawn and walked toward the flowerbed. "Hey, Ashton. Thanks for the coffee and cake. I'll let you know before I come in to repair the faucet."

She raised her hands to her forehead to cut out some glare. "You didn't say why you decided to show up early today."

He motioned as if to dismiss her question. "Let's just say I'm a workaholic, too.

"Sure, and I'll be here when you're ready to work on the faucet." Ashton shut the kitchen door behind her. Too bad the bee decided to buzz her right then. She wanted to hear James's story. Maybe she'd ask him another time. But then, maybe he didn't want to tell her since he changed the subject so quickly at the first mention.

And she'd sworn off workaholics.

JUNE FOSTER

Chapter Seven

James's pulse surged when Ashton strolled from the kitchen to the deck. Well, why not? Wouldn't a good-looking woman in form-fitting jeans and bright red t-shirt catch any man's interest? He propped the shovel against the elm's trunk and took a few paces toward her. "Morning."

"Thanks for fixing the faucet." Ashton descended the steps, paused on the lawn, and smiled. "Is there anything you can't do around here?"

James swallowed. *I can't fix the past.* He coughed a fake laugh. "Plenty. Like baking that delicious coffee cake you served me last week."

"There's more where that came from. You're welcome to breakfast anytime. My guests might enjoy the company."

He rubbed his stomach. "You got a deal."

She looked somewhere into the distance. "I've been here awhile and haven't taken a moment to walk the entire grounds."

"Let me go with you. If there's one thing I know, it's Gina's property. Did she ever tell you the legend of the missing gems?"

"Oh, I've been on many treasure hunts looking for those elusive gems before I realized it was a made-up tale." Ashton laughed.

"Oh, I don't know about that. Look at the home you live in. The original structure has been changed somewhat, but it's one of the most beautiful homes in the area. Look at the land they owned. The family was wealthy, especially for their time. The original owners were speculators and bankers. It's rumored that those seeking gold in California would barter anything and everything to make the journey. They even gave up true worth, like precious stones, even inheritances, because of the fever the hunt for gold caused."

"You said the original structure?"

"The inn has been remodeled and updated several times. I've read a little of the history of this area."

She smiled. "I'll do the same so I can share the inn's background with the guests, but Aunt Gina told me she had problems with guests showing up so they could actually sneak around and hunt for the gems."

He glanced around the perimeter of the yard. "Your neighbor to the north moved in a couple of years ago. You want to walk in that direction?"

"Let's start here and follow the path around the flower bed toward the azalea bushes."

"Sure." He started down the road. "Before you got here, it was covered in red flowers. You'll see next spring." But what would twelve months bring?

"A whole year running the inn. I hope I can make a success of it like my aunt did."

The trail curved around the elm where the stone marked Gina's grave.

Ashton touched her parted lips. "Oh." She gasped.

"More yellow roses. Did you leave them?"

"No. I figured you had." He leaned forward and sniffed. "These are fresh from a green house or floral shop. They weren't here Saturday, either."

They passed the fountain and headed toward the west side of the inn.

Ashton looked skyward. "What if whoever left the flowers did it in the middle of the night? It could account for the sound I heard. Maybe the muddy footprints were left there when the person meant to tell me so that finding the flowers wouldn't alarm me. I thought I saw a shadow pass the window while I was stuck in the shed." Even Ashton couldn't convince herself that she either was forgetful or crazy with fatigue. She had called out while in the shed. No one had answered her.

James looked around. "The ground is covered with grass here so we wouldn't likely see footprints. We could check with the local flower shop."

"Flower shop?"

James laughed. "There's only one. Cove Creations."

"It wouldn't hurt to ask."

"I'll go with you."

Ashton swung her legs around to relax in the passenger seat of James' car. He closed the door.

She had to admit. The guy's attention made her feel ladylike. She could get used to riding in the luxurious Lexus.

But how could he afford this car? Maybe a family member gave it to him. But then he'd told her nothing about them.

James pulled out onto the main road. "I'm sure the flower shop has a record of recent purchases. I can't imagine too many people ordering yellow roses."

"I've read they represent friendship, joy, and caring. Whoever left them must've cared a lot about Aunt Gina." She tapped her cheek with her index finger. "I recently discovered a charm Aunt Gina kept in a hidden compartment of a jewelry box. The inscription said, 'I'll always love you. RJ.' I wonder if RJ is still around and leaving roses on her grave."

James chuckled. "You mean like a boyfriend, or something?"

"Yeah. She never married, but I think there was someone in her life." She pursed her lips. She'd already failed in her promise to keep Aunt Gina's secret. "I'd appreciate you hold that in confidence for now."

"Yes, of course." He glanced at her with a half-smile then back to the road. "RJ. Hmm. She never spoke of anyone with those initials."

James made the left turn down Main past the administration office for Pacific Cranberry.

"I'd love to visit the bogs at the cove one of these days. Have you seen them?"

James tightened his grip on the steering wheel and looked away from the three-story building with the brick walls. "The flower shop is in the block next to the grocery."

Why did the question make him uneasy? In the next block, they pulled in front of Cove Creations with Washington's state flower, the rhododendron, above the words. He held the door for her as they walked in.

The lovely aroma of fresh flowers filled the air in the cool room.

A fifty-something woman looked up from the counter. "Hello, James. It's been a while. Where have you been keeping yourself?"

"Hello, Mrs. Carter." He glanced at Ashton. "This is Ashton Price. She's the new owner of The Inn at Cranberry Cove."

Mrs. Carter smiled. "Nice to meet you. Your aunt brightened our day when she came into the shop." Mrs. Carter cupped her mouth. "She always ordered yellow roses, her favorite."

Yellow roses? Ashton's pulse quickened. Aunt Gina certainly hadn't purchased flowers recently. But who? "Nice to meet you."

"Gina and I used to be friends in high school." Mrs. Carter leaned forward against the counter, her eyes sparkling with the memory. "We all graduated from Oceanview High. My husband Mike and I. Even Mayor Fernsby went there. We were in the same class and then all wound up in Cranberry Cove, if you can imagine."

James grinned at Ashton. "I'm not sure if you're familiar with Oceanview. It's a town about thirty miles north of here."

Ashton nodded. "When I was a kid, Aunt Gina talked about living there." But she'd never mentioned a boyfriend. "She always said, 'Ashton, enjoy every day of your life and thank God for the friends He places in your path. I made a lot of close ones in high school.'"

Mrs. Carter grinned. "Oh, honey. You remind me so much of her." She patted Ashton's hand. "We're so glad to have you in Cranberry Cove."

James lifted a finger. "Actually, we came in to ask you a question." He gave Ashton a quick look. "Could you tell us if anyone's ordered yellow roses recently. Someone placed some on Gina's grave, and Ashton would like to thank them."

Mrs. Carter squinted and pushed her glasses up on her brow. "Hmm. Let me see." She scanned her computer then looked up. "No, no yellow roses, but I'll let you know if anyone does. I usually catch up on the town's news at church. I'll keep my ears open."

"Thanks. I'd appreciate it," Ashton said.

Mrs. Carter focused on James. "Speaking of church. I haven't seen you there lately. You should come some time and bring Ashton. Actually, I haven't seen you since…" She let the sentence trail off as her face reddened. "I mean… I'm so sorry."

James grasped Ashton's arm. "I'd like to show Ashton around town a bit. Maybe take a ride to the ocean before it gets too late." He tugged her toward the door. "Thanks, Mrs. Carter."

On the sidewalk out front, James paused. "She's such a friendly woman. But if you let her, she'll talk all day."

Ashton slid into the Lexus. Granted, the floral shop owner talked a lot, but what had she started to say that made James uncomfortable?

Chapter Eight

Saturday morning, Ashton poured milk into the measuring cup. She added the liquid to the eggs with the butter, cheddar cheese and chopped ham then poured the mixture into the pan.

She set the carton in the fridge. Evergreen, a local business, had provided dairy products for as long as she could remember.

She flipped the omelet with the spatula and allowed the eggs to cook for another few minutes.

She loved when Aunt Gina use to take her to the dairy to see the cows, the silos, and best of all, the little shop where the owners sold homemade ice cream. She chuckled as she lifted the sides of the omelet. Aunt Gina always pretended they were going on a secret mission through the woods, following the trail from the northside of the inn to the dairy.

She scooped the omelet onto the plate and added garnishings of strawberries and peach slices then a piece of cranberry, walnut toast.

Yum. She'd better make another for herself since she'd offered James breakfast. She'd mentioned to the Claxtons last night that James would be dining with them this morning, and she'd looked forward to an additional guest, but they opted out, saying they wanted to get out of the house very early and do some sightseeing along the coast.

She grabbed a fork, a knife, and a napkin and set the plate on one of the side tables outside on the deck. "James, breakfast is served." She laughed.

James turned off the water at the faucet and took the steps up the deck two at a time. He grinned. "I want you to know I appreciate it. I've worked up an appetite, but weren't we supposed to join your guests?"

"They had planned an excursion today. I'm sorry you haven't been able to meet them. They're a very nice couple from California. But if I'm going to feed them in the morning, I need to get supplies." She pointed to the north behind the inn. "Do you know if the old trail to Evergreen Dairy is still there?"

James relaxed in the deck chair. "Yeah. I believe so. I used to explore the path when I was a kid."

"I'm surprised I never ran into you."

"I've changed." He snickered. "Used to be a skinny kid with holes in his jeans and tufts of brown hair sprouting from his head."

She laughed. "For old times' sake, I'd like to go over there and see if they still sell ice cream."

"It looks like a good day for a trek through the woods." James bowed his head then took a gigantic bite of eggs. "Umm. The omelet passes the test. It's delicious. If I didn't know better, I'd think Paula Dean concocted it."

"Ha." Ashton rolled her eyes. "I recognize flattery when I see it."

"No, really." James smiled.

"I'll leave you to the omelet. I'm going to buy some rocky road ice cream." She waved.

The trail at the north edge of her property led through a forest of Douglas fir. Yes, just as she remembered.

Low lying fern still bordered the well-traveled path. She inhaled a long breath of evergreen trees and wet pine needles. The sun, now overhead, filtered through the trees, sending shafts of light to the forest floor. In the distance, she recognized the barks of Mrs. Babbage small dogs.

Ashton's mouth watered with thoughts of the gooey chocolate including the walnut pieces and marshmallows. In about four hundred yards the trail would end at the backside of the dairy. Maybe she'd get two scoops.

Whispered voices met her ears. She stopped and turned to look around her. She could've sworn someone was nearby. She shook her head and continued the enjoyable walk.

The crack of a twig and the sound of a shush brought her to a dead stop. She might've convinced herself that a harmless animal trailed her, but the shush had most definitely been a woman. The fear that froze her thawed, and she turned to get a look at who could be nearby.

She was met by a blur of a figure too close to mean anything but harm. She closed her eyes and put her arm up for protection, cowering on the ground from any blow she might receive.

She screamed, the sound of it piercing the air as she turned away from her attacker.

She didn't dare look up to provoke her assailant

further. She lay there, shivering on the ground, the rush of blood filling her eardrums.

"Ashton! I thought I heard a scream."

Ashton dropped her arm and rolled over.

James raced toward her and grasped her hand to lift her up. "Are you okay?"

Ashton's knees wobbled beneath her, and she threw her arms around him and held on. "Someone rushed at me." She fought to keep the tears from falling. Warm arms encircled her before she realized how near he was.

"It's okay," he said. "You're safe now." His gaze circled their surroundings. "I didn't see anyone, but I wasn't looking. I thought maybe you'd fallen."

She pulled away, heat traveling to her face. "I'm so sorry. I didn't mean to…" She gulped.

"No, it's okay. I should've gone with you." James grasped her hand. "Let me walk you the rest of the way. A little ice cream can calm the nerves. The Taylors have the best anywhere."

James let her hand drop and walked in front on the narrow trail. At the clearing, the farm and the Taylor's home became visible. He waved at Mrs. Taylor in the yard, who stood next to her rose bushes.

She set the pruning shears down and met them. "Hello, there." She shaded her eyes with one hand. "James. James Atwood. How are things going at the inn?"

"Good. Nice to see you again."

Ashton moved next to him. "Mrs. Taylor. I'm Ashton Price. I'm not sure if you remember me. My aunt and I used to come through the woods from the inn to buy ice cream."

"Yes, of course. I was sorry to hear about her

passing. How are you, dear?"

"At the moment, I'm a little rattled. I was on my way here and had an encounter with someone. Did you see anyone come this way?"

Mrs. Taylor stepped closer to Ashton looking at her up and down. "Are you okay?"

Ashton inhaled a deep breath and rubbed her hip. "I believe so."

"I'm so sorry, but no one came through here. I've been outside a while."

Again, something had occurred, and she had no way to prove it to others. She couldn't claim fatigue because she'd gotten into a restful routine. She'd been able to sleep at night with the Claxtons nearby, but how could she explain these things? Ashton forced a smile. "Well, James said that ice cream is good for the nerves. We'd like some, and I need to get supplies."

"Of course, dear." The woman stared at James for a second too long, as if questioning Ashton. "Did you see anyone, James. Weren't you with her?"

"No. I was working in the yard. Ashton screamed, and I ran to help. I'm surprised you didn't hear her."

"No. I didn't, but I'm a little hard of hearing," Mrs. Taylor offered.

Ashton followed her to the small store next to the house.

"What flavor would you like?"

James gazed at the selection behind the glass display cabinet. "Hmm. Double chocolate with chocolate chunks."

"You're a chocolate lover, I see. I'll have rocky road." Ashton said. "The road here today was a little rocky, but I'm sure there's an explanation." There had to be an explanation.

Ashton just wasn't sure where she'd find it, though.

Ashton sat on the front porch enjoying the peaceful evening. James had just left, and the Claxtons were upstairs, settling in for an early evening, tired after their day's adventure.

A car approached and turned, parking in front of the inn. An older man, dressed in a suit and tie approached. He waved. "Evening. I suspect you're Ashton Price."

Ashton stood. "Yes, sir. Have you booked a room?" She had yet to open the reservations, working around the Claxtons to get everything in order, giving her some breathing room.

"No, ma'am. I'm Mayor Fernsby. This is just a social visit to welcome a new citizen and businesswoman to the community."

Had she broken some law, maybe she needed a permit. "Is everything okay with the business? I haven't done anything wrong, have I? I haven't officially opened, but Aunt Gina forgot about a reservation ..." She prattled on, afraid that she'd be fined before she'd even truly opened.

The mayor raised his hand. The smile he gave was a gentle, friendly one. "The inn has its permits, I'm sure. Your aunt was a long-time member of the Chamber of Commerce and the Better Business Bureau. Just remember to renew your licensing and to give your tax info." He winked.

Ashton relaxed and beaconed him to join her on the porch. "Where are my manners. I have some strawberry lemonade if you'd like to join me."

"No, ma'am. I just wanted to stop by and say hello and to make sure our newest citizen is acclimating to life in the small city."

Ashton fought the show of surprise. A mayor she'd never met sure seemed to know more about her than she'd expect. Maybe he was being cautious, making sure a criminal hadn't moved to town. She fought the thoughts that would lend themselves to more paranoia. "I actually like the small-town life, and I'm so glad you stopped by."

"Well, I was just passing by, and I saw you sitting here. You let me know if you have any questions or need any assistance. That's my job." He lifted his chin as if bringing home a point. Then he winked again. "I need to garner constituents, you know."

Ashton laughed. "Well, now, that's honest, and I like honesty in politicians."

The mayor's smile faded but returned just as quick. "You continue to enjoy this nice evening. I'm going to mosey on down this road." He walked to his car, looked back once he got to the door, and waved. Then he ducked inside.

Ashton watched him back out and drive away, and if she hadn't already entertained enough unproven conspiracy theories, she'd say the mayor had another reason for stopping by.

Ashton leaned back onto the down-filled pillow scented with lavender sachets. Tonight, she'd get a peaceful night's sleep. The Claxtons were nearby, and she'd convinced herself that she'd just stumbled upon someone who knew they shouldn't have been on the property.

She picked up the journal she'd planned to read for a week now and filled her lungs with a delightful breath. Gina. There were so many things she didn't know about her. Maybe the leather covered book would help.

Instead of flipping it open to a random page, she turned to the first entry.

April 1 – Junior year. Dear Diary, happy April Fool's Day. I'm not a fool, ha, ha. I'm almost a senior. Did I tell you? There's this boy who's so cute, but I don't think he even knows I exist. He's on the baseball team. All the girls are crazy about him.

Ashton grinned. A teenage Gina had fallen for someone. The floral shop owner said she'd attended Oceanview High with Aunt Gina. When Ashton had time, she'd hunt for Aunt Gina's high school yearbooks—possibly in the attic.

She turned a page.

April 10. Dear Diary, guess what. Today I watched RJ play baseball.

Ashton gasped. RJ. The initials on the heart-shaped gold charm she'd found in the jewelry box the day she took it to the bank.

He struck out three guys on the other team. Maybe he'll make it to the big league someday.

Ashton chuckled and flipped the page. Her youthful aunt had high expectations for this guy.

April 30. Dear Diary, I am so proud of RJ. He won the debate against the Olympia team. Maybe he'll be a politician someday.

With heavy lids and a smile, Ashton turned off the bedside lamp. She closed her eyes, visualizing a seventeen-year-old Gina. RJ must've fallen in love with her, too, but tomorrow she'd read more…

Someone or something sloshing through mud brought her from sleep. A light flashed outside. Lightning? No. She hadn't heart thunder. Terror propelled a cold chill down her back. Heart pounding, she tiptoed to the window. Darkness obstructed visibility. She needed to get a pole lamp for this side of the building.

Wait. Rays from a source of light skipped on the wet ground. There must've been a rain shower. Yes, now she remembered the patter on the window.

The light traveled toward the backyard. With sweaty palms, she turned the knob on the bedroom door and sneaked to the kitchen.

Dogs from the neighbor's house barked.

Perspiration immersed her like stifling humidity. The doors. She raced, checking the locks—the kitchen, on to the old chapel, and the front. She didn't want to awaken the Claxtons.

Should she call the police? If she did, word might get around that there were disturbances at the inn. Would it affect her business?

Again, she crept to the kitchen window, but she saw no sign of an intruder. She raced up the stairs to the second floor and peeked out the first room then to the other side of the hall. No light. Even the Claxtons went undisturbed.

Creeping down the stairs, she tiptoed to the apartment and tripped on a hairy creature.

He let out a howl.

"Sorry, Maxwell."

She locked the door, and he curled up on the bed.

Tomorrow. She needed to talk to James. He could help her. She had to buy a gun and then learn to shoot it.

Chapter Nine

Ashton turned over and glanced at the clock: 8:00 a.m. She shot up and rushed to the bathroom. The Claxtons usually rose early, and she'd overslept.

Maxwell lounged at the end of the bed, cleaning his fur.

"Hey, thanks a lot. You're supposed to wake me up when I oversleep. Aren't you hungry?"

She rubbed her eyes and retrieved her toothbrush. No wonder she'd overslept. She'd stayed awake an hour after last night's mystery visitor had called on her. The bouncing light and the strange sounds had unnerved her.

She threw on jeans and a t-shirt, brushed her hair, and tucked her cell phone into her back pocket. After she learned of the Claxtons' plans, she would need to call James.

She raced down the hall through the living room, Maxwell meowing behind her. She propped her fists on her waist. "Now you talk to me."

In the light of day, cowardness took a corner. She unlocked the front door and stepped out onto the porch. No signs of an intruder met her quick gaze. Yet something was off. She shook her head and started inside. Then she turned back.

The Claxtons' car wasn't in the drive.

Had she been sleeping so soundly after finally getting into dreamland, that they hadn't awakened her before leaving.

She shrugged and moved inside.

Maxwell met her with a meow of complaint.

In the kitchen, she headed for the backdoor. "Maxwell, before you say another thing, I've got to speak to James. This is important."

The sun shone today, casting sparkling beams on the Huckleberry bush beyond the deck as if no one had illegally entered the backyard last night. Ashton trekked from one side of the inn to the other, stopping beside the old chapel.

No signs of an intruder there either. She pulled out her cell. Beads of perspiration broke out on her forehead.

She clicked on contacts then her ringtone made her jump. The cell slipped from her hand and onto the thick grass. With a tightened jaw, she reached for the phone.

James's number flashed on the screen.

"Hey, James. I was trying to call you."

"I must have a bit of intuition or perhaps God made me make the call. I was worried about you."

She gulped hard.

"I'm going to take a little time out of my day and drive to Oceanview to pick up a new trellis. The old one's rotted out. I'll work on it tomorrow night. I expect a longer than usual day at this office today as well."

She tugged the edge of her t-shirt. "There's something I need—" No. If she told him, he'd head over. And everything else she'd claimed to have happened to her was just as unproven as the noises that awakened her last night.

"Something else you need from town?"

Not from town. She needed him—to help her figure out who invaded her home in the midnight hours, to investigate. Did she want to admit that something else may have happened? She needed his strong arms around her like the day on the trail to Evergreen Dairy. "No. No, it's nothing. I'll… I hope you have a good day. I'll see you tomorrow.

James stuffed his cell phone in his pocket and inched toward the mantel over the fireplace. He reached for the picture with the ornate frame and braced, proof that his life hadn't gone well.

He'd lied to Ashton. He knew exactly why he'd called her. She had been a good prescription for melancholy, and today, it fell over him like a cloak.

Lifting the photograph in front of his face, he forced himself to focus on the image of the child with light brown eyes the same color as his wife's.

Two lives cut short too soon. "God, why?" The question he'd asked hundreds of times, but God never seemed to answer. Never offered hope that someday James would find resolution for the way things ended.

He gently slid the photo in the desk drawer. Today would be hard enough without torturing himself with Sammy's image—or that of Sammy's mother.

He slammed his fist on the desk sending a wave of

pain through his arm. He'd promised himself he wouldn't go over this again. His marriage, his failure to make it work, burying himself in his job.

He was still keeping himself shoveled over with work and with the gardening at the inn. He had been able to keep these feelings at bay, and he needed to get going to his job.

He gathered his keys. Turning, he came face-to-face with his greatest obstacle. With a shuddering breath, he pushed open the door to the tiny bedroom, walked in, and slowly leaned back against the door until it clicked shut. Nothing stood between him and the boxes in the corner, but he couldn't move. Couldn't breathe for a second.

Then he inched forward. His son's life was summed up within the contents of two small boxes tucked in one corner of a much smaller home than the one in which Sammy had lived. He sank to his knees and pulled open the lid to the box closest to him. Sammy's clothes.

The little onesie James held in his hand was soft to the touch. He brushed it against his cheek and breathed in the scent of baby oil that reminded him of his son. He held it there imagining Sammy's soft hair resting against his cheek as he'd rocked him to sleep after a diaper change.

He didn't know when his sobs began, but his tears wetted the fabric. James wiped them with his hand, laid the onesie on the box lid, and pushed away.

He'd sure made a mess of things, and he'd lost so much.

What made him think he had the right to call Ashton Price and act as if he hadn't already messed up big with one woman who should've had his love and devotion and a child that had died because he'd been selfish.

On the front porch, James gasped for air. "You've forgiven me, Lord. I need freedom from the guilt," he bellowed, the words echoing off the fir trees across the road.

In his car, he attempted a deep breath. He couldn't expend all his energy on anger and sadness. He'd need it for the task ahead.

At the bend in the road, by instinct or perhaps even preference, he headed toward the inn then made a turn that would take him away from town. If he could only work in the garden today instead of taking care of what he'd let slide at work for far too long. Robert hadn't given him the information necessary to solving the dilemma, and yet another customer had called, unhappy with the distribution. He couldn't ask his clients the question that loomed large because he was afraid that it'd show that Pacific Cranberry, billed always as a family business, had a fracture in it.

James drove south toward the Pacific Cranberry bogs. Through the clearing in the trees, a bog resembling a pink carpet stretched in front of him. The berries wouldn't form until later in the summer.

No more procrastinating. Or had he just driven this way to remind himself what was at stake. He turned the car around and headed back to town.

JUNE FOSTER

Chapter Ten

At least Cranberry Cove had a Starbucks—though it was half the size of all of the Denver stores. Ashton didn't care as long as they had the blend of coffee she liked. She walked through the front door from the tree-lined, narrow sidewalk. Inside, the familiar earthy aroma of coffee beans and cinnamon, chocolate, and vanilla pastries made her mouth water. Besides a bag of beans, she couldn't pass up a caramel latte and a treat.

The display case with the myriad of pastries made it hard to choose. Cranberry scones, little donuts covered with vanilla icing, and pumpkin cupcakes.

"Yes, ma'am. May I help you?" A young woman whose nametag said Gracie grinned at Ashton. With her red hair, freckles, hazel eyes, could she be any prettier?

"How about a cranberry muffin and medium latte with almond milk?"

Gracie nodded, her curls bouncing, and bagged the muffin. "You're new in town, aren't you?"

"Yes, I'm Ashton Price, the owner of the inn on the east side of Cranberry Cove."

"Nice to meet you. I'm Gracie Mayberry." She

glanced up and smiled. "My mom used to work for your aunt before she passed away."

Thoughts of a redheaded woman with Gracie's features sparked in her memory. "Oh, yeah. I remember her. She used to let me fold towels. Mrs. Babbage told me about your mom, and I didn't remember, but seeing you ... you favor each other."

Gracie poured two shots of espresso into a cardboard cup and filled it the rest of the way with the steamed almond milk. "I wish you much success with the inn. So many people loved your aunt." She twisted a lid on top.

Ashton sipped from the cup and glanced at the poster on the wall. "The Founder's Day Parade. I didn't realize they still had it."

"Yes, it's coming up in three days. You should go. Starbucks has a spot this year."

"Great. Maybe the inn can sponsor one next year. Could be good for business."

"We applied with the city council, but Mayor Fernsby is a good person to contact as well." She glanced toward the door and lowered her voice. "Speaking of him, he just walked in. Let me introduce you."

The handsome man Ashton had met previously entered. He had been distinctive before, but now the streaks of silver highlighting his hair gained her attention.

Gracie grinned. "Mr. Fernsby, I have someone I want you to meet."

He held his shoulders back, and a genuine smile broke out. "Good morning, Ms. Price. Good to see you again so soon." He shook her hand and then turned to

Gracie. "I'll take my usual, Gracie."

"Coming up, Mayor." Gracie poured milk into the small stainless-steel container. "So, you've met Ashton? We were just talking about her sponsoring a float in next year's Founder's Day Parade."

The mayor's eyes teared. "Oh, yes. I'll be happy to secure a place for you." He whipped out a handkerchief and wiped his nose, his eyes blinking as if the bright lights in the room blinded him. "As I told you, we're very happy to … er have you in the community." He stared at something over her shoulder. "We miss your aunt more than we can say."

We? Or did he mean he missed her?

The man seemed overcome with emotion. "On second thought, I'll skip the latte today. I just remembered a meeting." He turned toward the door.

"What got into him?" Gracie stared after the mayor.

Ashton shook her head. "I don't know."

James stared at Robert, unable to believe the man's blatant disregard for James's request. "What do you mean you haven't had time to look into it? I want the information, and I've been patient enough."

The door to Robert's office opened and Dad peeked inside. "Everything okay in here, boys?"

Robert stomped around his desk. "Uncle Rodney, I've had about enough of James. The way he's intruding on my work, you'd think he has none of his own."

"James, marketing isn't keeping you busy

enough?" Dad asked.

"I'd say that I have more than enough to keep me busy, but Robert isn't returning customers' phone calls, so Leslie and I are doing double duty, taking complaints about non-deliveries and invoices charged for non-existent inventory." James didn't lift his gaze from Robert as he spoke. "And when I asked Robert to dig into what was happening at the warehouse with distribution—his job, I might add—he refused."

"Nothing's happening." Robert shrugged.

James crossed his arms over his chest. "That nothing has cost us three accounts while I waited for Robert to find something."

Dad rubbed his hand over his mouth. "Robert, is there a reason that you haven't taken the calls?"

"I haven't received any!" Robert raised his voice. "I suspect that Leslie's behind this."

James heaved a heavy sigh. "For the last time, Leslie is my secretary. She's only acting on your behalf because you can't keep anyone."

"Boys!" Dad raised his voice just as he often did when James and Robert fought as children. "Aren't we ever going to get beyond this petty squabbling?"

"This isn't a squabble, Dad. We're not kids, though I doubt Robert has ever truly matured. If he isn't going to do the job the company pays him to do, and if I have to do it, then I suggest that he be let go."

"Let go!" Robert laughed. "My family owns this business just as much as yours."

"Robert, son," Dad stepped forward and placed a firm hand on Robert's shoulder. "Our family—we're all one family—owns this business, and if what James is saying about your work ethic is true, I expect you to pick up the slack. If we've lost three accounts, you need to find out why. Now, James, I suggest you step back. You've had a lot of trauma in your life, and it can make us impatient."

James bit his lip. To tell his father that he'd given Robert more than adequate time was a waste of breath. He'd already explained the three missing accounts.

"Everything okay in here?" Uncle Terrance stepped into the office. "You boys at it like old times?"

"Excuse me." James stepped past his father and his uncle.

Leslie was on the phone, but she hung up as he approached her desk. "Tomorrow morning," he looked over his shoulder, making sure his voice could be heard, "if we have no report from Robert by close of business today, I'd like to talk to someone from the warehouse, maybe the production manager." He lowered his voice. "If that report isn't given to me, make a note to contact the production manager as soon as you arrive to work and set the appointment for 9:30 a.m."

"Yes, sir, boss." Leslie gave him a salute.

The evening had arrived, and as usual, the Claxtons had not returned. Since their arrival, they'd eaten mainly breakfast. On occasions, they shared a dessert with her, but otherwise, they ate elsewhere. Ashton strolled out onto the deck.

James's car was parked out front. She hadn't seen him arrive though she'd been watching, hoping he could provide more information about the Founder's Day Parade, and she had decided to mention the midnight noise.

She took the path toward the elm and Aunt Gina's grave. Ashton gasped. Fresh yellow roses filled the container—again. Whoever brought them seemed to deliver new ones in the middle of the week.

Perhaps she needed to fence off the area. Though the roses were nice, the backyard of the property wasn't public ground.

She continued toward the west side of the yard. James wasn't trimming bushes there.

Meandering along the north end, she neared the shed. Beyond, the lawn extended to a section of yard with the gorgeous garden of rose bushes of every shade from pink to deep red.

An unfinished trellis was propped against the back of the shed.

James dipped a brush into white paint and sloshed it onto the wooden fencing.

"Hey, James. The roses are looking great."

He turned to her. "While I was in Oceanview, I got that trellis I told you about yesterday. It'll work for the climbing blue roses. I thought I'd give it a coat of paint."

"They're gorgeous." The exquisite bush was full of blooms. "How much did the trellis cost?"

He stood and set the brush on a tarp he'd spread under the trellis. "No need to reimburse me. There's still ample funds in Gina's maintenance account."

"Okay, if you're sure. I need to keep a running total of your expenditures, though. For tax reasons."

"Of course. I shouldn't have tossed the receipt in

the garbage, but I'll give you a written one later."

She ran her finger over the smooth, glossy petal of one of the roses. "Do you know anything about the Founder's Day Parade?"

"Yes. I believe they began holding the parade in the last fifty years to commemorate the founders of the town and the town itself. We should enter next year. Since June is the best month for roses, we might want to incorporate that theme."

They did think alike. "Did Gina ever sponsor a float?"

"Several times before her health declined. Why don't we go together Saturday? You'll like it."

"Sounds good." She took a long breath. "Another thing. I believe someone's skulking around this place at night. I was awakened, but when I've looked for any evidence, I can't find it."

He gripped her shoulder. "Ashton, why didn't you call the police?"

She ran her hands through her hair. "I have to be careful with my paying guests here." Though, if the truth be known, she'd been unable to track their payment. She hated to ask the couple. They'd caused her no problems at all. Except if they were non-paying, she was rendering services at cost to herself.

"Even so, your safety is most important." He peered into her eyes. "Please, promise me you'll call 9-1-1 next time."

She sighed. "I promise."

The sound of a shrill, loud voice resounded from the east side of the property.

Ashton froze. Was someone in trouble?

James laughed. "Mrs. Babbage."

"What's wrong? Sounds like she's screaming at someone."

"Naw. Don't worry about her. She hollers at the deer who come up to her property and eat her bushes. She has a fence but the creatures seem to get in anyway."

Gina snapped her fingers. "Speaking of Mrs. Babbage, I met Gracie Mayberry at Starbucks."

James stopped painting. "What does Mrs. Babbage have to do with Gracie?"

Ashton shook her head. She'd forgotten her train was on a different track from their earlier conversation. "Mrs. Babbage mentioned that a Mrs. Mayberry used to work for Aunt Gina. I didn't remember her until I met Gracie. Hard not to forget that red hair. I suppose when Aunt Gina passed, she lost her job."

James visibly tensed. "Mrs. Mayberry is cleaning house for several people since leaving the inn. Your aunt had employed her fulltime. Then she found another fulltime job with someone else."

"Do you know if she'd be willing to work with me again when I'm ready?"

James smiled now. "I can't speak for her, but she might be open to the prospect of returning to work here. Let me know when you think you'll need her."

"I'll have to see if the reservations roll in when I'm ready to open up completely."

He tilted his head and studied her. "Ashton, you already have guests. Of course, I haven't seen them …" he raised and lowered his brows. "Is there another reason you're procrastinating?"

"I'm still doing some cleaning," she offered. No way would she admit the truth. Either she was losing her sanity or something was going on at the inn that she didn't understand, and she wasn't sure that it didn't pose a danger to others.

Chapter Eleven

James made his way toward his office.

Leslie held up a sticky note with the reminder to call the production manager. "Jacob will arrive promptly at 9:30 a.m."

James hitched a thumb toward his cousin's office.

Leslie chuckled. "Yeah, right. He's been sauntering in around anywhere between 10:30 a.m. and 1:00 p.m."

"Any mention that he'd have the report, even if it is late?"

She shook her head. "He only talks to me to ground out orders."

"I'm sorry for that, Leslie, but right now having you working for both of us is strategic."

"I gotcha, boss. I haven't wanted to say anything, but several employees think something's going on. A few are worried."

Leslie wasn't one to gossip, so he wouldn't push. While he'd like to blame Robert for all the troubles, he had no real proof. Dad and Uncle Terrance were slowing down. They hadn't said anything, but James felt sure that one or both of them would announce retirement.

Where that would lead was anyone's guess, especially if James couldn't work out his differences with his cousin. He suspected that the only reason their fathers had not retired was a fear that the cousins would tear the business apart with what Dad referred to as squabbles. Yes, they'd never gotten along, and as adults, they'd maintained as much distance as possible.

This distribution issue had brought James into Robert's world, and James couldn't say he was comfortable with that.

At 9:30 a.m., on the dot, Leslie knocked on James's door and showed in Jacob McKinley. The man wore a ball cap covering his brown hair. He took it off as James offered him a seat and held out his hand. "Hey, man. Good to see you."

The manager of Pacific's production plant gripped his in a shake and pushed his glasses up on his nose.

"How's everything going on your side of the company?" James didn't want to jump right into the reason for the visit.

"Actually, I was glad to receive Leslie's call. We need to talk." He swiped his hand over his mouth. "I'm worried about the business."

Good for Leslie. She did have a pulse on the company. "Anything specific?"

"James, we've known each other a long time. You know I've never been inclined to pass on tales, but things need to be said."

"What made you think I wouldn't be willing to listen to anything you felt troubling?" James sat back. "My door has always been open."

"Your door ain't the door to distribution, and that's where I believe the trouble is." Jacob leaned forward and lowered his voice. "Your dad and your uncle are always talking up the family side of the business, and I had to believe Robert when he told me I'd be fired for addressing any issues I had. He said, and I quote, 'the old men would fire you for suggesting there's a problem.'"

James stood and closed his office door that Leslie, as was their habit, left often during conferences. In all the time he'd worked with Jacob, he never known him to exaggerate or pass on rumors. James wouldn't call his cousin a liar. James had trouble getting his father or his uncle to see problems. They seemed to think that anything negative reflected on the family. "I'm listening."

Jacob ran a hand through his hair and plopped the hat on again. "I got my information firsthand from your cousin's previous secretary and the warehouse distribution manager who deals with him almost every day." Jacob looked to the left then the right.

Uncertainty stirred in James's stomach. "Tell me."

"They believe that Robert is basically trying to undermine the company. He's been overheard declaring he'll be president soon."

James gave a half-laugh. He never expected he'd have to fight for the position, but if meant keeping the business running smoothly, he'd be ready for war.

"Anyway, once word got out about that—" Jacob clamped his mouth shut.

"Jacob, Robert is well aware that I'm having this meeting with you today. I've asked him to clear up several discrepancies having to do with distribution and invoicing. I'm reaching out to you first to determine what's going on with the warehouse. I have a feeling, you're about to tell me a few of your concerns. Believe me. I'm not doing this because there's family infighting. I'm doing this because I have a family and our family has a family of employees that depend on Pacific Cranberry. I have to resolve these issues before I can try to win back the accounts we've lost."

"That's just the thing, James. The reason people are talking is that Robert's mouth and his actions aren't meeting up in the middle, if you know what I mean."

"Why don't you explain it to me?"

Jacob paused to run his hand through his hair again. "Everyone's asking the same question. How does Robert expect to become president of a company he's running into the ground? You mentioned invoicing? Rumor has it that Robert uses accounts like they belong to him. The billing department jokes about it. Everyone sees when he pulls in and when he leaves. They see you working your butt off—and I'm glad to know you don't stay here until all hours of the night and on weekends since ... well, since you lost your family."

The man had been holding a lot in, and James refused to take exception at the remark. After all, he had spent his married life mostly in his office.

Jacob didn't seem to notice that James's mind had wandered. "If Robert gets the position, especially if he gets it over you, you'll lose half your employees. I know that for a fact. They expect he'll run this place into the ground in less than a year, and where will that leave us? Think what those job losses would do to our community." Jacob gritted his teeth and sat back as if remembering where he was. "I'm sorry. I got myself all worked up wondering if Robert wasn't the reason behind my being called in today. I thought I was getting fired, and I came determined to have my say. I guess I exploded."

James steepled his fingers together and studied them for a long time. "I owe you an apology."

"No, you don't. Everyone knows you get us the accounts that keep us working. Robert's supposed to maintain those accounts. You said it yourself. We're a family at Pacific Cranberry. I couldn't see your dad or your uncle actually firing us for a complaint, but that blowhard—I'm sorry—your cousin, he has a way of twisting the truth and laying the blame on others. He's really good at intimidation. I should have known I could come to you."

"Can I ask you a few favors?" James stood and waited for Jacob to do the same.

"Anything short of illegal." Jacob winked.

"Can you do your best to quell the rumors about a change in presidency. Truth is, while Dad and Uncle Terrance are nearing retirement age, we haven't talked about this at all. Robert is saying things that haven't been discussed with him or with me. That should shut down the fear caused by his careless words."

"Done."

"Can you give me information on the distribution of these three accounts?" James handed Jacob a list he'd had Leslie prepare before Jacob's arrival. "Were deliveries requested? Who took the order? Were the deliveries made? Were they cancelled and by whom?"

Jacob read the sheet and handed it back to James. "I can tell you those deliveries were requested. I can get you the name of the girl in the office who took the order. Each time I had the order ready for delivery, it was cancelled. I don't need the office to tell me by whom. Your cousin stopped those orders."

James fought hard from showing any surprise. "Good work. And yes, if you'll have the distribution office send me the date and time the order was placed along with any information they may have on whether the stores canceled the delivery, I'd appreciate it."

"I'll have them check for a cancellation from the store, but I'm sure we won't find one."

"Because Robert told you directly?" James asked.

Jacob lowered his head and peeked out from under his hat. "I'm dating a girl in billing. After that third cancellation, I kind of spilled that filling trucks with stock that wasn't going anywhere really wasn't my favorite thing to do. My girlfriend said that Robert had made sure she billed the companies for the orders. She wanted to know why I hadn't sent out the delivery?"

James leaned against the doorframe. "I really wish both of you felt you could come to me or to my dad or my uncle. But I can understand why you didn't." James held out his hand. "This is between you and me, Jacob, but before you unload any further cancelled deliveries, you let me know, and please ask distribution not to speak about this particular company business. You can understand why."

"Yes, I can." For the first time since Jacob had met with him, he smiled. "I'll take care of things, rumors, and information. You just make sure that cousin of yours doesn't run us out of business. As you said, we're a family."

Jacob exited, and James stepped out into the hallway. Leslie answered his unasked question with a shake of her head. Robert had not arrived. "Get billing on the line for me, please."

JUNE FOSTER

Chapter Twelve

Even as a kid, Ashton loved parades. The clarinets' toots, the trombones' blares, and the repetitive taps of a cymbal sent goosebumps down her arms causing her to shiver. Though she hadn't attended school in Cranberry Cove, the high school kids in their blue and white uniforms made her proud. Main Street likely hadn't seen this many people since the last Founder's Day.

Next to her in the folding chair, James sat up straight. "Cold?" He peeled off his jacket and wrapped it around her shoulders.

Not only his coat but his smile enveloped her in warmth in the cool morning breeze. His soft blue eyes drew her in, filling her insides with wonder. A sensation she hadn't expected. "Thanks."

James shaded his brow with one hand. "Starbuck's float is coming up behind the band."

Featuring green and white balloons, the platform rolled into view.

"Whoa. Look at that giant paper coffee cup. It must be six feet high. Some mornings I could use one like that." He laughed.

"There's Gracie. You can't miss her with all that curly red hair."

Gracie tossed a gift card toward Ashton.

"Hey, how come one of those other two girls didn't throw one to me?"

Ashton lifted her chin in mock superiority. "I guess I'm special."

Firefighters on a bright red antique truck blew the siren, and Ashton stuffed her fingers in her ears. Behind the firetruck, a brigade of at least twenty school children sporting Cranberry Cove Elementary School t-shirts rode their bikes and screamed at the sound. "Do it again," one called out.

She had to admit, having James by her side felt good. Though she still didn't know much about him, he wasn't the midnight intruder. His obvious love and respect for her aunt proved it.

Yet he held something from her. In time, when he was ready, he'd open up, wouldn't he?

He looked her way with a smile and back to the parade. "Hmm. This day takes me back to childhood. I used to come with my parents—" He snapped his mouth shut as if he'd said too much.

"I'd like to hear about them." Ashton wrapped his coat tighter around her taking in the aroma of a wood fire and soap. "In fact, you never told me where you work during the week."

He shrugged. "They still live in Cranberry Cove, and I see them on occasion. Not as much lately."

The fact he didn't answer her question about work was very obvious. She poked him. "I hope I'm not over working you at the inn." Maybe that would give him a hint of her curiosity.

"No, no, it's not that. Dad's usually busy." He looked toward the Pacific Cranberry float down the street. Had he deliberately misread her question?

Ashton held out her hand when one of two teenage girls tossed a nutrition bar into the crowd. "That one has dried cranberries. I bought some at Hometown Market the other day, and they're delicious. Our town is fortunate to have the company headquarters here."

James pointed across the street. "Look at those three kids waving miniature American flags. One thing I like about the parade here is that it's family oriented."

Did he just avoid talking about Pacific Cranberry? She folded her arms over her chest.

Another band in red and white uniforms from Oceanview High played the school's fight song then the snare drums tapped out a rhythm.

"Aunt Gina's alma mater."

James nodded. "There's our esteemed mayor. Can't say enough good about him. He's been a boon to our economy since he was first elected and has always supported local businesses."

"Did I tell you he stopped by the inn to welcome me to town?"

"No. But that sounds like him."

Mayor Fernsby waved from the driver's seat of his older model Lincoln convertible, flashing a smile as if he'd come straight from Hollywood. His red and white jersey with Oceanview Seadogs on front made a statement. Though Mayor of Cranberry Cove, he supported his hometown high school team today.

"The Seadogs are Oceanview's team names. I believe he once told me he lettered in baseball," James said.

Baseball? "I recall something about that, but I can't remember what." Ashton waved at the two teens sitting atop the backseat wearing Mr. and Miss Cranberry Cove High School sashes.

The mayor glanced her way. He seemed to startle for a moment, but then he offered her the warm smile he'd bestowed upon her before.

She tapped James's arm. "I also ran into him at Starbucks, and if I didn't know better, I'd think he'd started to cry. Just now, he seemed surprised to see me."

James scratched his head. "I heard he and Gina used to be an item in high school, but it could only be a rumor. Maybe you remind him of her, and he wants to forget the past." He shrugged. "Just a guess."

An odd thought struck. "What's his first name?"

"Roy. Roy Fernsby. That's the way it appears on campaign posters, the newspaper, at the ballot box. He's serving his second four-year term now. Why do you ask?"

"RJ." She murmured. It had to be him.

"What did you say?"

Ashton shook her head trying to make sense of it. "Remember the charm I mentioned. The initials on it were RJ. Aunt Gina also wrote about RJ in her diary. She mentioned he was a pitcher. I wonder if it could have been the mayor."

"RJ?" He squinted. "I believe his middle name is Joe."

James grasped Ashton's hand as they bypassed a mud puddle and arrived at the large parking lot behind the bank where he'd left his car. Having her by his side brought comfort, and with it a sense of contentment. He didn't want to believe he was attracted to her. Not after so short a time. But he could stare at her beautiful face and green eyes for hours. Did he dare to admit she'd begun to fill the lonely gap in his life?

A sense of disloyalty overwhelmed him, and he slammed his hands in his pocket. Bethany had been dead for less than two months, and already he'd looked at another woman. In reality, though, their marriage had died long before that infamous day.

"James, look over there at the other end of the lot where the floats are parked. Mayor Fernsby. I want to say hello."

The only problem with that right now was that the mayor was having a conversation with two people he wanted to avoid—his parents. He hadn't told Ashton about the business. He told himself that he didn't want her to be worried he was working too hard. Lately, though, he wondered if there wasn't another reason he'd kept it quiet. He was still running away from his problems, and he didn't want anyone else to know.

"Come on," Ashton urged.

"Right now?"

She hiked her hands on her waist. "I want to ask him about Gina. This may not be the best time, but I've got to find out. Do you suppose he's the one bringing the roses? It only makes sense. They were in love in high school, and his initials are RJ."

"Yeah, but the mayor was married for a long time—and it wasn't to Gina. His wife was an ancestor of the founder of South Fork, the county seat. They later moved to Cranberry Cove."

"He was married?"

"Yes, she died a few years ago."

"But why would he marry someone else if he was in love with Gina?"

James grinned. "Ashton, it was a high school romance."

"Sometimes first loves are meant to be together."

He'd have to disagree. He and Bethany...

Ashton pinched her lips. "Well, I intend to find out more."

Spunky. Ashton wasn't a quitter—one of the things he admired about her, but right now, her ambition was intersecting with his need for privacy. "Okay, let's walk over there." This would be interesting.

They walked to where the mayor stood by his car talking to James's parents. Around them, parade participants began to dismantle the floats and band members, instrument cases in hand, boarded a yellow school bus.

"Hey, Ashton." From beside her float, Gracie Mayberry smiled. Another intersection he didn't want to cross. He'd told a half-lie to Ashton about Gracie's mom. Mrs. Mayberry had worked for him after Gina's death. She'd kept the estate up until he'd sold it. Feeling guilty for having to let her go, he'd offered her a job at Pacific Cranberry, but she refused, saying she liked keeping homes in order.

"Hi, Gracie. Great job." Ashton waved then stopped in front of the mayor's white Lincoln.

"James." His mother stepped forward and straightened his shirt. Then she turned her full attention to Ashton. "Hello, I'm Marie Atwood, James's mother."

Ashton gave him a quick glance, her eyes widened. "Oh, hello."

"Mom, Dad, this is my friend, and I've recently learned, a friend of the mayor's as well, Ashton Price. She's Gina Price's niece, and she's the new owner of The Inn at Cranberry Cove."

"Oh, Roy!" Mom slipped an arm around Mayor Fernsby as if to offer him comfort. "Doesn't she look like Gina."

The mayor nodded without speaking, emotion playing on his face.

"Now, Marie," Dad coaxed. "That's very ancient history. That was when you all attended school together. Asking Roy to remember what Gina looked like would be like asking me what Mary Ellen Bonner wore to my senior prom."

Mom leaned back in mock anger. "And just what did Mary Ellen Bonner wear to your senior prom, Rodney Atwood?"

"A pink strapless number that made me blush." Dad laughed. "But that's beside the point."

The mayor touched Ashton on the shoulder. "You definitely do remind me of your aunt. It brought up ancient but good memories. Now, if you'll excuse me, I do need to attend to a few things." He started to walk away but stopped. "Perhaps you wouldn't mind if I called on you real soon. I could tell you some stories about your aunt."

"I look forward to it," Ashton must've picked up on the mayor's unease in a way his mother hadn't.

The mayor turned to James's parents. "Perhaps we can get together for dinner soon."

"I'd like that," Dad agreed.

"You take care." The mayor nodded and walked away.

"We were just headed to get a quick bite," Mom, ever the polite one, said. "Would you two like to join us?"

"I have some work to get done," James said.

That was more than a subtle hint to his mother that the discussion was over. Even James knew that was the way he stopped conversations he didn't want to engage in. He'd exchanged life for work every time he couldn't face things head-on. So far, that'd be most things.

He tugged Ashton's arm, and she followed after him without question.

And for reasons he couldn't quite grasp, he understood that asking her to leave without accomplishing her goal of talking to the major was very, very wrong.

Chapter Thirteen

Leslie met James in front of his office door, blocking it. The frown she wore told him that his Monday morning was not going to start well.

James tilted his head, peering at her. "What's going on."

"This afternoon is the final game for my son's little league baseball team." She took a long breath. "All the other kids have fathers who go, but Timmy doesn't. The game starts at three thirty. Robert dropped a big project on me this morning—yes, this morning. He's already here. I explained that I would work around anything you gave me, but I am leaving for Timmy's game. He said I had too much to do, and if I couldn't separate my family life from my work life, he'd make sure all I had was my family life." She covered her mouth, tears in her eyes. "It's hard being a single parent, James, and to have him—he really can't do that, can he? I mean you gave me the time off. Can he fire me if I go to the game?"

James stood and placed a hand on her shoulder. "I was a parent for less than a year…" Now he wished he hadn't verbalized the thought. Nor could he imagine raising a child alone, though he'd give anything he owned to have Sammy back. James shook off the thoughts.

Leslie gripped her hands. "You understand, right? I work hard for Pacific Cranberry, for you and for Robert, but my boy has to come first."

James blew out a breath. "We can't claim that we're a 'family' company if we don't recognize the needs of the families of our employees. Timmy needs you. You leave in enough time to get Timmy to the game, and you enjoy that game. You don't miss a precious moment of your son's life." James swallowed hard. If only he had heeded that advice. Dad had stood in James's office doorway many a night, coaxing him to go home to his wife and his son.

Robert exited his office. "I thought I heard you." He glared at Leslie then to James. "I suppose she's telling you a sad tale about not being given the permission to take off early. Leslie's quality of work has decreased a hundred percent in the last several months. She doesn't deserve any favors right now—not until she can prove herself worthy of the standards Pacific Cranberry has held for years."

James took Robert by the elbow and led him away from *his* secretary. "Leslie does your work only because I asked her to do so. The prerogative has always been hers. You should be thanking her. She doesn't run when treated with disrespect by you. She will be leaving when she's ready to take her son to his game." He marched back to her desk and searched for anything that looked like Robert's demands. He found a stack and started to pick it up.

Leslie rushed back to her desk and took the papers

from him. She gave a short shake of her head. "James, it isn't that I mind doing the work. Robert has some warehouse forms he wants me to review." She nodded toward his cousin. "If you don't mind waiting a day or two on the project you asked for, I'll do my best to get Robert's done. If I can't finish before I leave, I'll complete the work first thing in the morning."

Leslie was doing her job—and doing it well.

James turned back to Robert. "Does that meet with your approval? I have no problem with her postponing my work. Are you going to concede, or do we need to take this matter to the company president?" He hated pulling rank because Robert's insecurities were fed by the fact that Rodney Atwood and not Terrance Atwood acted as president, but Robert wouldn't want to have this debate. Dad knew that Leslie worked for James.

Robert's scowl softened. "Okay." He turned to Leslie. "Go to the game, but please don't make shirking your job a habit."

Leslie waited until Robert shut his office door. "Thank you," she muttered.

James wasn't done with Robert, yet. He marched into his cousin's office without knocking. Robert slapped his office phone back on the receiver as if James had caught him in the act of doing something wrong. "I wouldn't blame you if you went after a woman like Leslie. She's pretty hot." He chuckled. "Got something going on with her, cuz?"

James huffed. "Leslie's a loyal employee and a friend. Nothing more than that."

"That's right. I heard. You got a thing going on with Gina Price's niece. Carrying a torch from one Ms. Price to the other, I see."

James stepped forward. "That's a sick insinuation made by an even sicker mind. Gina Price was my friend. She helped me through a hard time. So, yeah, I'm returning a favor for her niece, helping her take care of the place."

"Interesting."

"How so?" James demanded.

"You never were that keen on helping your own wife. You didn't stay at home long enough to let her know you cared. In fact, I know she definitely thought you didn't care for her. Bethany was miserable with you."

James sucked in a breath. Other people knew of their problems?

"In fact, rumor has it you were on the verge of leaving Bethany high and dry. Of course, she had ready and willing arms that helped her through it. Someone who really loved her. I showed her that."

James grabbed Robert's shirt collar and shook him. "What did I do to make you hate me?"

Robert jerked from James's grip and brushed off his shirt. "You have that hot stuff degree and don't mind flaunting it. You married the woman I loved, and then you neglected her." Robert clamped his lips shut, as if he wanted to retrieve the words.

James clutched the edge of Robert's desk. "What?"

"You heard me. I loved Bethany, but she only had eyes for you. Later, she was sorry she married you. The times we were together, I showed her what she missed."

"You slept with my wife?" James fisted his hands.

"Yeah, what of it? You were too busy to care."

James trembled before his cousin, fighting hard the urge to punch him. Fear that one punch wouldn't be enough drove him toward the door. Robert could be lying. He wasn't known to tell the truth often, but he had hit upon one certainty: James had not loved Bethany as he should, and he hid behind his work to keep from dealing with the truth. Whether Bethany had actually been foolish enough to turn to a man like Robert, he didn't know.

"You may have gotten the education, but in the end, before she died due to your lack of concern, she said she loved me. She was coming to me. Don't you ever forget that. The day she died, Bethany was coming to me."

James held to the doorjamb and turned a pointed look at his cousin. "If that's true, Robert, you carry just as much blame as I do for the loss of Bethany and the death of my son." He shut the door softly.

Leslie started to move in his direction, most likely hearing the entire conversation. James held up his hand and headed for the door. He needed air. He needed soil. He needed something to take away the pain from him.

Ashton switched off her computer, stretched her arms behind her, and strolled out onto the deck. The overhead sun warmed her cheeks. Cooped up all morning with her work, she needed fresh air before she started a new mission.

The Mayor—RJ—was Aunt Gina's first love—and likely her last. She'd never have guessed his identity, but she could understand why her aunt fell for the handsome, ambitious guy. Had he been as good looking in high school?

Aunt Gina's yearbooks. She'd promised herself for days she'd look for them. Were they in the attic? She didn't relish going up to the dusty, dark loft filled with spider webs. Next time James had some spare moments, she'd ask him to help her.

Ashton stepped inside again and glanced around the kitchen. On second thought, Aunt Gina hadn't stuck them away in some remote location like the attic. Having the memories at her fingertips sounded more logical. But where?

The long hallway off the entrance had several closets which she'd meant to go through. Ugh. They contained boxes that'd take hours to investigate. In a couple of days, she'd explore them.

Though it was close to sunset, she still had time to take a walk. In her apartment closet, she pulled out a pair of tennis shoes and stepped out of her sandals.

A blue plastic box sat on the top shelf. She'd noticed it before but hadn't checked it out.

She stood on tiptoes and reached for the box, setting it on the floor. Folding her legs under her, she sat on the throw rug and slid the top off the container. What looked like mementos from high school lay inside. Yes, this had to be what she was seeking.

Ashton pulled out a sweater with the Seadog emblem on the front, a small box with a girl's graduation ring, a stuffed dog in a red and white sweater, and three yearbooks.

Heart pounding, she set the sophomore and junior years aside and opened the one displaying the date of her aunt's senior year. She flipped through the pages and stopped at one entitled, "Most Likely to Succeed."

Gina's picture was accompanied by the quote, "I want to own a place where people can enjoy a meal and an overnight stay."

Ashton scanned a few of the other titles. Farther down, she saw "Most Likely to Go into Politics" with a picture of a young RJ. She chuckled. He'd fulfilled the prediction, but why had he run for office in Cranberry Cove? Could he have followed Aunt Gina here? Maybe Ashton would never know. She replaced the box on the closet's shelf.

Tennis shoes on, she locked the entrance door. The manicured front lawn, the trimmed shrubs, and the flowerbeds filled with color gave proof James had the outside ready for visitors.

James. Last Saturday at the parade, he'd avoided speaking about his job, and he hadn't seemed very happy for her to meet his parents. He'd shared very little with her.

She took Rose Garden Lane in front of the inn. At the curve where the name changed to Main, Hemlock Way veered to the left. Just for fun, she followed the county road. Since James said he lived south of the inn, maybe she'd spot his cabin.

Fir trees lined the road as the forest grew thicker. The aroma of damp moss and wet tree trunks thickened as the landscape changed into lush woodland. If James lived down this way, he must've enjoyed the setting.

She paused. A bird's sound held her captive. Ka-ka-kow-kowlp. The yellow-billed cuckoo she'd read about a few days ago in a local magazine.

Ashton checked her walking app. Two miles.

To the right, a small cabin nestled among the trees, and a Lexus was parked in front. This was a weekday, and he was home. Did he work from home, or had he taken the day off?

The cabin was built of logs except for the rock fireplace. The home must've been constructed in the early 1900s or even before. A long ribbon of smoke trailed from the rock fireplace.

Curious about things James hadn't told her, she slowly stepped toward the house. What would he think if she knocked on his door? She continued until she reached the porch stretching across the front. Her blood pressure skyrocketing, she raised her knuckles then froze. She couldn't. He might think her an idiot, or worse, some kind of a stalker.

Her face flamed. What if he'd seen her? Turning back, she scurried down the steps and onto the road. Though she wanted to see where James lived, she couldn't appear to be spying on him. Her courage to learn more about James failed her now that she was definitely in his territory.

James took another bite of the chili he'd heated up for lunch. One day was all he needed. One day when he didn't have to come face to face with Robert. He promised himself he'd return tomorrow.

He took his empty bowl to the sink. Maybe he could go to work at the inn early, but Ashton had been so skittish with things she couldn't explain. He didn't want to show up unannounced during the day. Well aware that he'd used the inn as a substitute for work at the office, he decided he didn't care. It offered him the peace he needed to face the office, or more particularly, Robert, these days.

Movement outside the kitchen window caught his eye.

What? Ashton paced down the steps in front of his cabin. Had she knocked, and he didn't hear her? Why was she here anyway?

He opened the door and called. "Ashton, are you okay?"

She stopped and turned around, her face red. "Oh, James. I was out for a walk. I ran across your house."

"I can see that," he teased. "Come in, please. We need to talk."

"I…" She frowned and walked up the steps. "It must be serious given the look on your face."

"You don't have to pretend. You know I've been avoiding telling you certain things, and one of those things is about my time at the inn."

"You can't come back. I understand." Ashton fiddled with the edge of her t-shirt. "I'm sorry. I hope I didn't do something…"

His phone rang, and he lifted his index finger. "Please sit down. I need to take this." He slumped into the kitchen chair. "Thanks for calling me back, Dad."

"Your message said you had something serious to talk to me about, but Leslie said you weren't here today."

"I needed to get out for a bit. I'd like to meet with you tomorrow."

"It's good to hear that you're taking some time. You took a day last month, son, and I was relieved. Enjoy the rest of your day. I'll see you tomorrow."

"I'll be there early." He clicked off the phone and

stuck it in his pocket.

Ashton sat in the other kitchen chair wide-eyed. "What—what did you want to talk about?"

"Let me get you a cup of coffee. This may take a while." The moment had finally come. Ashton had to know.

Ashton sipped the earthy brew James offered her. The cup warmed her icy hands, not cold from the weather but from what James would say next. She feared he was quitting his job at the inn. She set the cup on the old metal table and swallowed hard.

James trained his gaze toward her. "First, I need to apologize. There's something about me that I should've told you sooner. I wasn't being fair to you."

A tight knot began to grow in her stomach, and she clenched her fists. "No problem." She lifted her chin to look out the window. "You're not obligated to share anything about your life with me."

"No, Ashton. It had nothing to do with you."

She folded her arms over her chest. "All right. I'm listening." From the dark circles under his eyes, obviously a difficulty had arisen.

"Let me start from the first. I haven't always been Gina's gardener."

"I figured as much."

He cracked his knuckles. "Pacific Cranberry, whose business office is downtown on Main, has been in the Atwood family for generations. My father is the current president." He stared at her as if waiting to see her reaction. "I'm the VP of Marketing.

She tossed an errant strand of hair out of her eyes. "Why did you think that keeping it from me would matter?" Although the thought of his working all day and then arriving at the inn after work and on Saturdays did seem a lot for him to handle.

He coughed hard. "Because of the reason I do the gardening and handywork at the inn. Yes, Gina was good to me at a time when I needed it, but I have other reasons."

"The treasure?" Was she in danger? Was he about to tell her the truth, because he'd found the gems and didn't want anyone to know? "Are you the person whose been doing all these things?" She pulled back.

He stared at her and then laughed. "No. I can honestly tell you that I am not looking for the gems. It never occurred to me. Gina hired me to work in the garden because she knew it took me away from the office. It's still work, but it isn't the same as staying at the office until all hours and full weekends."

"Perhaps you're a workaholic," she stated the obvious. "Is the inn a distraction?"

He shook his head, running his index finger along the edge of his cup. "I suppose it's stupid, but part of me said if I ignored the problems in my life, they would go away. I ignored them by staying in my office."

"Are you trying to tell me that you're going back to working less hours, that I'll need to find someone else for the work around the inn?" She couldn't afford another gardener, but would she find time to do it herself? "I understand. You have to take care of yourself first."

He covered her hand with his—maybe for the last

time. He wouldn't work at the inn much longer.

"I would never abandon Gina's garden—or you. I plan to continue working evenings and weekends."

She wrinkled her forehead. "But won't you wear yourself out?"

"I haven't so far. The work I do at the inn is refreshing. I'm outdoors. I can sleep at night. "The garden is a sanctuary—where I find God's peace, His strength. Please, Ashton. Don't worry about your yard."

"James, what problems are you running from?"

James stared beyond her, to a closed door. "My recent past. The things that I should've done but I stayed in the office, and I failed to do them. They cost me a lot."

"I don't understand."

He slipped his hand under hers and stared at it. "Would you allow me a little space on that right now. I'll talk to you about it, but I recently got hit hard with something, and it's opened a fresh wound. I was about to call you to let you know I planned to work at the inn. With all that's going on, I didn't want to frighten you if you saw me in the yard and didn't know I was there. Seems, from your accusation, that I might have been right to call."

"I'm sorry about that." The warmth crept up her face. "Mrs. Babbage's talk of ghostly lights and things happening when no one else is around or when the Claxtons are asleep, they have me on edge."

"Lean on me a little, then. Don't think for a moment I don't believe you. If I thought you were crazy, I'd tell you."

"Oh really?" She leaned back, the smile coming without effort.

"Yeah, like just now when you accused me of being a treasure hunter. That was a little crazy."

Coward. Coward. The word shot darts into James's chest, reminding him. He was fumbling around, avoiding the whole truth, and Ashton deserved to know. Maybe he could open up a little more. He stood. "Follow me."

Ashton lifted her brow, never taking her gaze from him.

James sauntered toward the closed door where he'd hidden his precious treasure, a treasure so costly to him that it hurt too much to gaze upon it. There was no sense in rushing. In moments, she'd know about Sammy. Steeling his nerves, he opened his mouth. "I'd like to show you something."

"What is it?" Ashton's frown spoke more of confusion than suspicion.

He took a breath, allowing time to get himself under control. He entered the room and stood over the boxes until he sensed Ashton had joined him. Then he reached down and picked up the blue one-piece his son had worn when he was around seven months—the one James had cried into the first time he'd looked at it since he'd moved here from the estate. Then he reached into the box and pulled out a pair of baby shoes and set them on the unmade bed.

Ashton clasped both sides of her face, her mouth open. She moaned. "James, did these things belong to your child?"

He raked a hand through his hair and nodded. "My son's name was Samuel Atwood. I called him Sammy." His voice hitched. He thought he could get a momentary handle on the grief, but he guessed he couldn't.

"When did you lose him?"

James took another breath then gave himself a stiff mental kick in the rear. *You've dealt with the loss. It's time to let it go.* "Sammy and his mother died two months ago."

Ashton placed a hand to her throat. "His mother?" She had apparently grasped the implications of his statement. "Two months."

James reached for her hand and led her back to the kitchen table. "Sit down." As he feared, the look of pain on her face mimicked the others around town when they thought they were offering condolences. They felt sorry for him. But he didn't deserve it. "Bethany and I were married for five years. Two months ago, when Sammy was almost a year, he and Bethany were killed in a car accident. A semi plowed over them."

Her features softened. Pity. He couldn't bear pity. He didn't deserve it. If she only knew the entire truth. "I'm so sorry." She covered his hand.

He slowly pulled away. If he told her everything, she'd have no compassion for him.

And he needed Ashton. Especially now.

Chapter Fourteen

James walked into the 1920's style building housing Pacific Cranberry, passed his office, and went straight to the breakroom.

Leslie poured a splash of cream in her mug and looked up. "James." She grabbed her coffee and headed toward him. "I was worried about you. I couldn't help but hear what Robert said. I think he wanted everyone to hear it. Are you okay?"

He pushed a smile into place. "I've lived with my cousin all my life. He has always liked to say shocking things to get a reaction from me."

"But is it true?"

No matter what had happened between James and his wife, he would not betray Bethany in any way. "I won't believe the worst about my wife." At least that was the truth. He'd decided that when he'd returned from the inn last night after working himself so hard, he could only shower and fall into bed. He hadn't told Ashton anything about his marriage. Still a coward, but at least she knew he'd been married, had been a father, and the reason he worked so hard. She didn't need to know how bad his marriage had been and what he'd done.

"So, how'd the project for Robert go? Did you get it done or are you still working on it this morning?"

"Oh, I got it done. By the way, I took the liberty of ordering lunch in for the billing department today. They stayed a little late so they could confirm some things for me. I found the papers on my desk when I arrived this morning. You'll see that I found concrete proof of my suspicions." She stepped to the breakroom door and back. "I placed their report and my full report on your desk. You know, Robert thinks I'm his secretary. You asked him for a report he never delivered. I kind of felt badly about not helping him. "Her sly smile told him she'd found something to hang the man who treated each of his secretaries as if he owned them.

"I should have a look at that report. I appreciate your compliance with my request."

"Hey, you're my real boss. I'm glad to be of help." She moved closer to him. "The thing I can't figure out, James, is why he's doing what he's doing. It's like he's destroying the business that provides him a paycheck—and rejecting his own family. I know that you've never taken more than your salary from this business, and you'd never harm your dad or your uncle, but Robert …" She stepped back. "James, he has to go."

James pushed past her without a word. He needed to find out what his cousin was doing and take appropriate action.

Two hours later, he rubbed tired eyes. He'd look through Leslie's report and then through the corresponding documents she'd tagged to show that Robert was not only embezzling from the company—more than taking a little from the till as Jacob called it—his cousin was doing something that perplexed James as much as it had Leslie. He was destroying relationships with businesses James had fostered for years.

He thought about going to see his father and his uncle right away, but they would only think it a petty squabble between their two sons. Instead, he started his calls. Robert had worked to destroy relationships with three accounts. Since James's edict to Jacob, Robert had not stopped a shipment or Jacob would have reported it, and nothing showed in the report. Only the three businesses had been sabotaged so far.

Two more hours later—an entire morning spent on cleaning up what should be a smooth-running operation—James had promised the companies that the invoice situation had been cleared and taken off the books, and that if they would accept the gift from Pacific Cranberry for their inconvenience, he would assure that they received the next shipment free of charge. He refused to blame the girls in billing, but he also didn't want their customers to know that there was a problem in the Atwood family. He simply advised that he'd been looking into the matter and promised it wouldn't happen again.

The people he dealt with had been stern, disappointed in the company at first, but as James worked his magic, they softened their attitude.

He picked up his phone and asked Leslie to come into his office.

She entered with her notepad, ready to take orders, and sat at the chair in front of his desk. "Yes, boss."

"First question: he in?" James pointed to the wall behind her, indicating Robert's office.

"Not yet."

"Second question: would you mind putting up with him for a little longer?"

"Whatever you need."

He took a deep breath. "I have assured our fine customers who were treated so badly by our Vice President of Distribution that they would"—he nodded toward her notepad—"receive a free shipment of the order that was not delivered to them as promised."

He'd worked long enough with Leslie that he knew she understood he was giving her a list of jobs to do.

"I also promised them that the invoices would be cleared from billing and that our work practices would improve such that this would never happen again. When you contact billing and finance, I'd like you to tell them that should Robert enter their office for any reason, and should he ask for a check or take one cent from the till, they are to call me…" He eyed her. "Or you."

Leslie nodded. "I understand."

"I don't think you do." He leaned back and stared up at the ceiling for a long moment. "I am unofficially appointing you as unofficial Vice President of Distribution with all the authority that goes along with it, including stopping any leaks, whatever they may be."

"Kind of like a shadow vice presidency?" She smiled.

"Exactly."

She grimaced. "I don't like it, boss. I'm being shoved in the middle of an Atwood issue."

She was right.

He made a face and leaned forward. "You're going

to force me to talk to them, aren't you?"

She laughed. "Yeah, I am. I believe even a shadow vice president needs a raise."

James laughed aloud and pointed at her. "You set that hook and reeled me right in." He stood. "I'll get you that raise and take the stress of being in the middle away from you, but I need you there. Do you understand?"

She stood and saluted before leaving the office. "Would I be pushing it if I asked for an extra week of vacation?"

For all she did, she wasn't pushing anything, but he wasn't about to tell her that.

Next order of business. Talk to Dad. James walked down the hall and found his Dad sitting alone in the conference room. He knocked and walked inside. "Are you having a meeting?" he asked.

"Just with your uncle to discuss sales. We have a few minutes. What's on your mind?"

James pointed to the door. "May I close it? I'd like to talk in private."

Dad frowned. "Go ahead."

James slipped into the seat. "Dad, I need to tell you something that may be difficult for you to hear, but I'd appreciate it if you'd hear me out."

Dad startled a bit but nodded.

"We lost three accounts recently due to a lack of distribution."

Dad waved his hand. "Robert isn't good at his job, but he's family."

This was the obstacle he knew he'd meet. Family was everything to the elder Atwood brothers. That's why he had to take a different tact. "I'm glad you admit that."

"Now, James, I'm not going to entertain letting him go. He has just as much right to this company as you do."

"Fair enough." James forced himself to relax. He had one opportunity to slip his secret weapon into play, and he had to go about it smoothly. "I've spoken with Leslie. She's a little reluctant to do as I ask without yours and Uncle Terrance's permission, but I have an idea that will help Robert to become more efficient. Would you like to have Uncle Terrance join us?"

"And Robert?" Dad asked.

He had to work this through without Robert. "You'll admit that Robert can be temperamental if his abilities are challenged, and I believe that Uncle Terrance will see what I'm trying to do as something good for Robert." Like keeping him out of prison.

Dad picked up the conference room phone and asked Uncle Terrance to join them.

His uncle entered a few minutes later, smiled, and clasped James's hand. "I noticed you've been taking some time off. Good for you. Now, what are we here to discuss?"

Dad raised his hand. "We were about to discuss the loss in percentage of sales, but I think James unwittingly discovered the reason."

"Is that so? What is it we need to change, James?"

Uncle Terrance was such a good man. He trusted James, and that's why he had to do things this way—for the family—his parents, his uncle and aunt, Robert, and the Pacific Cranberry family. "I learned that three very loyal and consistent accounts hadn't received deliveries, yet they'd been invoiced *by mail*." James waited for the exact force of what he said to seep into the thought processes of the two men. By sending a fraudulent invoice via mail, Robert had committed a federal crime that could impact the company.

Uncle Terrance pulled out a chair and set down. "I suppose this is something that required Robert's attention."

"Yes sir. I asked him for a report. Leslie, who is filling in as his secretary, prepared that report for me when Robert gave her some work to do. She basically completed the report for him and found some discrepancies. I have the report if you'd like to see it. We can track the placement of the orders, the fact they were set for delivery, and Robert cancelled each order on the day they were to be delivered. Then Robert told billing to send the invoices. The warehouse thought the orders were cancelled by our customers. Billing believed the customers received the goods."

Uncle Terrance lowered his head and nodded. "No. I trust you. He's inattentive to his job. He's making ludicrous decisions, and he takes too many liberties as a member of this family."

"Terrance," Dad said his brother's name softly. "I believe James is trying to tell you that by billing for items not received, the company, if this matter had not been rectified, could've accused us of mail fraud."

James hadn't wanted to be that blunt, but he could understand a parent's inability to perceive the worst in a son. "Leslie's report impressed me. Since she's been working for Robert, she's learned the ins and outs of distribution."

"You aren't suggesting we fire Robert—?"

Dad's defenses were up.

James needed to bring them down.

"Rodney, let's hear what James has to say. I get the feeling he's trying to offer us a better solution."

Had Uncle Terrance overheard the conversation with Leslie, or did he really believe the best in James. If he believed the best, James was disappointed in himself. If it was up to James, Robert Atwood would be in jail.

"Go ahead, son," Dad urged.

"Robert has his way of doing things. We're very different in our work tactics, but Leslie is willing to fill in when Robert isn't available, to oversee things for him."

"A shadow vice presidency, I believe it's called," Uncle Terrance winked, giving up his charade. "And it's a very good idea."

"I don't understand." Dad shook his head.

"It's simple, Rodney. My son has harmed our business. James is attempting to save Robert's reputation and our company at the same time. We've allowed Robert this long to roam free. He doesn't do his job. We need someone to do the work. Leslie is very capable. She's willing to do it to help us. And that loyalty needs to be repaid. James, she gets a vice president's pay, and because she doesn't get to own the title, and she's doing more work than the one holding that title, she gets two extra weeks' vacation."

"But …but…?" Dad stuttered.

Uncle Terrance stood. "I know you're the official president of this company, and I rarely, if ever, make decisions without you, but trust me on this one, your son is acting in the best interest of the Atwood family." He turned to James. "And if you'll ask Leslie to report any friction with my son while conducting her new duties, I will have occasion to address the issues with him without letting him know what's really going on."

James stood and waited for his dad to clear the decision.

Dad gave him the nod.

James walked down the hall and toward Leslie's cubicle. She eyed Robert's office, a silent message that his cousin had finally arrived to work. "Thank you for all your hard work that you do for me and for Robert." He leaned toward her. "Not only is everything cleared, Uncle Terrance is onboard. Any disputes that arise, we are to take to him."

"Honestly?" Leslie widened her eyes.

He leaned closer and lowered his voice. "Your paycheck will reflect your new secret position, and you are granted two extra weeks of vacation."

She gasped. "Really?"

He held up his hand.

She gave him the high-five. "I won't let the family down."

Ashton turned out the light and closed her eyes. She'd thought of nothing else but James since yesterday afternoon. How he must've suffered. She understood now why he didn't want to talk about his past. Aunt Gina must've been a great source of comfort to him.

For over an hour, she tossed, unable to get James's story out of her mind. She turned over for the hundredth time but stopped. Had that been a noise? Maybe the

Claxtons were up having a late-night snack. They'd arrived back rather late. She sat up and listened.

From outside, she heard a splash, as if someone toted a bucket of water and it sloshed over the side. Then someone or something stomped, she was sure, on the deck.

Heart pounding, she threw on her robe, grabbed her flashlight, and tiptoed to the kitchen door. She shone the beam through the window. No one. She flipped on the back-porch light and inched outside.

A pail James had used to fill the birdbath lay on its side. Water had spilled on the deck's wooden surface. Could a raccoon or deer have milled around out here? No. Animals usually didn't come up as far as the deck.

That was it, all the proof she needed. A prowler was after something at the inn, but what?

The back-porch light flicked on. "What's going on out here?" Oggie stood in the doorway.

Ashton jumped. "I heard a noise."

"Yeah. Got that." He looked over his shoulder and back. "You see anyone?"

"No, but someone must've fallen over this bucket. They probably realized it would wake someone."

"Yep. Pretty sure that happened."

If Ashton didn't know better, she'd think he was being sarcastic.

Beatrice poked her head over Oggie's shoulder. "You okay, honey?"

"Yes." Ashton headed back inside. "I think I need to call the police. Just to be safe."

"No." The word left Oggie's lips like a command. "No need to do that. We can take care of anyone who comes around."

"I appreciate your wanting to be the protector, but I need to alert them in case someone comes around again." She grabbed her phone from her room and punched in 9-1-1, coming back to the couple. "Yes, there's an intruder at The Inn at Cranberry Cove. Please send a patrol car."

She put the phone away.

"We're going upstairs." Oggie stomped up the steps, Beatrice following. "Good night."

"But the police may want to talk to you."

"You just tell them that your guest told you they saw nothing."

"But you heard the noise. You saw the overturned bucket."

"You can tell them that as well as we can."

Ashton watched them climb the rest of the way up the stairs and then into their room.

In twenty minutes, she opened the front door for two officers. After a complete search of the grounds, they only found tire marks on the west side of the inn but no signs of entry. They assumed she was alone at the inn and didn't ask if anyone else had heard or saw anything. Not wanting to disturb the Claxtons, she didn't mention them.

Still, their attitudes when she had called the police left her unsettled.

She let the officers out and returned to her bedroom, a cold sweat running down her back. "Decision made," she muttered. "Tomorrow I'm going to ask James to ride with me to Oceanview. I need his opinion on the best weapon I can find to protect me from intruders outside and from any future guests who might not be who they claimed."

And she was beginning to wonder about the Claxtons.

James pulled out of the Oceanview Shooting Range, grateful Ashton had asked for his help. "I can't imagine what the prowler is after, but I'm glad you called the police. I think you'll be happy with a Smith and Wesson. After the paperwork clears, you'll be ready to use it because the range had the similar gun for you to practice on."

"I hope you weren't too tired after a long day's work."

"It's my pleasure." Being with Ashton shooed away the stressors of the day. Her friendship infused him with refreshing energy and purpose. If only they could avoid focusing on the past and perhaps a friendship in the future. "While we're here, we might as well go down to the beach. If you'd like."

"Yes, sounds perfect."

In ten minutes, James turned off at the sign. He lowered the window to listen to the roll of the waves. In the distance, the ocean's sea green tint reminded him of Ashton's eyes.

Within seconds after he parked, she jumped out of the car and raced toward the water. "I love the beach. I never got to go when I lived in Denver." She giggled.

Though Uncle Terrance had been on board with James's actions, the tension of having his uncle face the truth about Robert had lingered. In Ashton's presence, that angst melted away as he shed his shoes and chased after her, enjoying the feeling of sand between his toes. "Hey, wait up." When he arrived at her side, he grasped her hand.

She looked up at him with a smile.

Sandpipers, looking for dinner, followed the tide as they hurried toward the ocean.

"Are you sure that I'm not causing you undue stress? I don't know how you handle both jobs."

He wanted to explain why he had to work at the inn, what it did for him—especially in light of Robert's betrayal—but now wasn't the time to trust her with company or family business. Both were so intertwined; he couldn't separate them. "I don't consider what I do at the inn work. It takes me away from the stress."

"I'm a good listener if you ever need one."

He paused, planting his feet in the sand.

The woman before him, as well as the thrashing of the ocean washed away concern over the company's future. He grasped her elbow and turned her to face him. The feel of her velvety skin on his fingers heightened his awareness. She was so near.

He shouldn't. But he only listened to his heart. "Ashton," he whispered. He leaned closer to her plump lips. The aroma of the fresh strawberry scent of her shampoo elevated the pounding tempo in his veins. He couldn't resist. The rhythmic waves urged him on.

A phone buzzed, and he stepped back.

"Oh?" Ashton reached for her cell. She stared at the screen and chuckled. "Not the best time for a spam call."

JUNE FOSTER

Chapter Fifteen

James's attention shifted from the computer to his office window. The greenbelt of pine and fir heartened him more than usual. His fingers rested on the computer keys as a distracting thought kidnapped his concentration.

A week now, and he still treasured the memory of his and Ashton's walk on the beach and their *almost* kiss. Maybe loving her meant the beginning of a new life. If only he could leave the past behind and receive God's forgiveness.

He shook off the musings and peered at the computer screen again, rechecking the reach of their latest marketing endeavor. The information was hard to analyze because the three companies he'd been able to win back after Robert's actions had received free shipments. Any additional orders would come within a week or two. Still, a follow-up call to assure the free deliveries had been made would send the message that Pacific Cranberry valued its customers.

Thirty minutes later, he hung up and pushed away from the desk. All locations indicated receipt of the deliveries, and James had forwarded their calls to the appropriate office for placing additional orders.

Disaster avoided. Leslie was doing Robert's job like a professional. Unfair, though, was the fact that she was also helping him and maintaining a façade as Robert's secretary. That ruse was necessary to provide her with a shield. After all, she was acting on Robert's behalf, making things easy for him. Since Robert's only interest seemed to be in destroying the company, and Leslie was standing sentinel, Robert had to be fuming.

James trudged down the hall to Robert's office. Leslie had indicated she needed to walk over to finance, and now would be a good time to get a gauge on Robert's thoughts. He knocked on the door and waited. After several more taps, he walked in leaving the door open.

"Talk soon." Robert hung up the phone. "Should I be honored you've finally graced me with your presence?"

"No need for sarcasm. I wanted to see if everything was okay. You and Leslie were a little at war."

Robert stared long and hard, and James could almost imagine his cousin weighing his next move. "Nothing's changed. She's underachieving, as usual."

Time had come for James to share a little of his knowledge with Robert, but he had to be careful to keep Leslie out of the middle and to put Robert in the corner where he needed to be. His cousin's pride would help James do that.

"I appreciate the report. Late or not, it gave me the information I needed to find out where our problems might be."

"Report?" Robert jolted.

James tilted his head. "The report you sent me.

Leslie cc'd Dad and Uncle Terrance. They both were impressed with what you'd found."

Robert covered his mouth for a fierce cough. "Well, yeah. It had to be straightened out. You need to follow up more closely with your accounts to make sure that anything that happens at the warehouse and in accounting doesn't hurt the business."

James couldn't resist his smirk. Robert. What a jerk. "I agree. I'll be much more attentive." To say the least. "I had to jump through a number of hoops to get the three companies I allowed to slide back into the good graces of Pacific Cranberry." Sarcasm laced his voice. "Your efficient report helped us to do that."

The report Leslie had forwarded only included the distribution and invoicing information, not the billing office's report on how much money Robert thought belonged to him alone. But Dad and Uncle Terrance had been handed that information as well.

The key to everything was to let Robert know he was being watched. James had done his job.

"Well, maybe it's time to make a few changes." He rose from his desk and advanced within three inches of James's face. "Like who's going to run this company in the future."

James did his best to act surprised at Robert's announcement. Jacob had already informed him that Robert intended to become president. If his cousin had been as steadfast and had maintained the same work ethic as their fathers, James would've had no problem with the appointment. Now, though, he wouldn't let that happen. "So, you think you can handle the job?"

"Better than you. If you can't handle life's ups and downs, how can you handle a company like Pacific

Cranberry?"

Of all the low-down ... James gritted his teeth so hard his jaws ached. "Are you referring to the death of my wife and child as an up and down of life?"

"We all experience unfortunate situations, but that doesn't give us license to shirk our responsibilities." A sneer crept across Robert's mouth.

"I'd think that given what you said to me about your relationship with my wife, you might consider my loss more than a little bump in the road. Or perhaps I can take what you said for what I know it to be—a lie meant to bait me."

Robert grabbed James's shirt and tugged. "Listen... "

"You two stop it." Uncle Terrance stormed through the open door. "I heard you down the hall." He looked to James. "You are aware one does not have to eavesdrop to hear any conversation louder than normal."

James nodded. "Yes, sir. I'm sorry to have raised my voice."

"So long as we're clear. We don't need others overhearing family issues." He turned to his son. "I don't know what you've previously said to James, but I have to agree with him. Your behavior toward him in the wake of his grief is not something I will ever condone."

Robert had to know that his father had subtly demanded Robert give James an apology.

Robert moved around his desk and sat down. "Just so he knows, he almost cost us three accounts."

"Son!"

"No, Uncle Terrance. It's okay. I handled the

issues. I followed up with our customers. That sort of thing isn't going to happen again. I've placed safety measures in play to keep me from ever letting our customers down again."

Uncle Terrance patted his shoulder. "I can't ask for more."

James exited, and Uncle Terrance followed. Each headed in separate directions without a word.

Robert wasn't a dunce. He had to figure out that he was in a world of trouble if he stepped out of line again.

Ashton walked into the city library. Finally, she had a moment to accomplish the task she'd put off. At the information desk, a young woman with long dark hair peered at a computer screen.

"Hi. Could you point me in the direction of local history? I'd like to learn more about The Inn at Cranberry Cove. I'm the new owner."

The librarian's face brightened, and she stuck out her hand. "I'm so glad to meet you. I knew your aunt. She was such a dear."

"Thank you. I'm hoping to carry on the work she started and would like to know some interesting facts I can tell visitors."

"On the far-left wall, you'll find books about the history of Cranberry Cove, some by local authors and others historians who wrote about our region."

"Thank you so much." Ashton turned to walk in that direction.

"The place fascinates me," the librarian said.

Ashton turned toward her.

"I plan to stay at the inn when you open."

Joy leapt to Ashton's throat. Her first potential customer—not the Claxtons who were there by default. "I'd love to have you." She smiled.

"From what I've read, the inn's original owners were well-to-do bankers. Cranberry Cove was the perfect place to be because of the California Gold Rush. People went insane with gold fever."

"That's what my aunt used to tell me."

"There's a tale about the inn that's been passed down since the 1800s. A wealthy young man came through town on his way to California from the east coast. The journey had almost cost him all the funds he had with him. He fell in love with the banker's daughter, but the banker, not realizing the man came from a wealthy family, forbid his daughter from courting someone who would be leaving town. That's when the man brought forth a bag of rare gems that he'd carried with him and kept secret by sewing them into his coat for the journey. He offered them as a pledge to the banker and his daughter that once he returned with more gold to increase his family's wealth, he would wed the young miss. He only asked that the man keep the jewels and not sell them and asked for enough money to get his supplies and to see him on his way. The banker gave of his own money for the young man's journey."

Ashton leaned on the counter, enthralled by a part of the story she'd never heard. Aunt Gina only knew the banker had obtained gems from a man on his way to California, and because they were never turned over to the bank or found in the home, she had assumed it to be a made-up tale.

"The man never returned, but rumors started that the banker had provided bank funding for the man but kept the collateral for himself. But I've done some research. This man and his wife were Christians, and they were very good to the community. I believe the account of his personal funding to be true."

"So, what do you think happened?" Ashton asked.

"I believe the banker paid for the supplies out of his own pocket. I haven't made up my mind if the banker sent the man away knowing the dangers of the journey or if he expected him to return. But his daughter never married, and they say she always stayed true to the young man she'd fallen in love with." The librarian slapped her hand against the counter, startling Ashton. "And I believe that the lights people have seen at the inn since your aunt passed are the ghosts of the young couple who finally had the home to themselves." She smiled and leaned forward. "Mark Twain said it this way, 'You don't have to believe in ghost to enjoy a good ghost story.'"

"My neighbor, Mrs. Babbage mentioned the lights. You say others have seen them?"

The woman smiled. "Mrs. Babbage is a regular at the library. She told me. I believe folks were taking advantage of an empty place to do a little treasure hunting."

And that might be who was causing Ashton such a fright.

"Well, it's a good thing I don't believe in ghosts." Ashton smiled. "Thanks for the history lesson and the ghost story. I can tell you there are no ghosts at the inn."

But something strange was definitely going on.

Chapter Sixteen

Ashton stepped onto the deck, eased into one of the yard chairs, and set her coffee mug on the side table. James definitely kept the gardens manicured and lush.

Late yesterday afternoon when he'd planted new flowers and weeded the garden, he didn't seem tired. Working all day at a corporate job then coming to the inn might've worn her out. But she had to believe him when he said he enjoyed it—as if the garden offered therapy.

The memory of the beach that day lingered. Some might think it too soon for James to hang out with another woman, but it wasn't any of their business. The guy seemed to want to move on. Why not give him the chance? She had to admit—she would've welcomed his kiss. Next time she'd turn off her phone.

Ashton glanced toward the break in the trees. Mrs. Babbage, the spry little woman who couldn't weigh over a hundred pounds, made her way toward Ashton, a dessert plate in her hand. The woman had lived up to her promise to provide delicious desserts.

"Yoo-hoo, Ashton. You have a visitor out front."

Mrs. Babbage stopped and cupped her hand to the side of her mouth. "Mayor Fernsby, she's in the back."

Footfalls on grass soon led to the mayor coming into view. "I hope I'm not interrupting you ladies."

"Good morning, Mayor?" Ashton stood and took the dessert from Mrs. Babbage. "Thank you so much."

"I told you dear. It keeps me busy." She teared up as she always did. "Gina was so good to me to let me be a part of the inn in some way. She and Mrs. Mayberry and I would sit out here some evenings and just enjoy a light conversation."

"You are always welcome." Ashton slipped an arm around her. "And, please, I know you keep saying it isn't necessary, but it would be no problem for me to pick up and buy any ingredients you need."

"No, dear." Mrs. Babbage waved her off. "I'd love to stay and visit now with you and Mayor Fernsby, but one of my four-legged children has a date at the spa." She giggled. "Mayor, you'll have to try one of my lemon tarts."

"Yes, ma'am," Mayor Fernsby smiled. "You drive careful now."

Mrs. Babbage hurried off.

"Am I interrupting your day?" the mayor asked.

"No. Let me take this inside. Would you like to try one of Mrs. Babbage's tarts? They really are good."

The mayor patted his stomach. "I just had lunch, but maybe I'll take a raincheck."

Ashton hurried inside, sat down the dessert platter, and reached in the refrigerator for strawberry lemonade. She poured two glasses and ventured back outside to the deck. "It's such a fine afternoon. Do you mind sitting outside?"

"No. Nice days like this are meant to be enjoyed." He sat.

Ashton took the chair beside him. "I believe you said you had some stories to tell me about my aunt."

The mayor took a drink. "You didn't know we were old friends?"

Ashton shook her head and sipped her lemonade.

The mayor remained silent. A smile was absent on his face.

"My work kept me away from Aunt Gina most of the time. When she was sick, she didn't really let her family know the severity of the cancer. She kept it quiet from us when she stopped the treatments. Her funeral was a blur for me. I don't recall any of those who attended."

He nodded and swiped his hand across his eyes. "She could be stubborn like that. Never wanted anyone to help her carry a burden."

So, Mayor Fernsby did know her aunt well. "I want to give you full disclosure, though. I found something that led me to discover that you knew my aunt. I mean, I didn't know it was you until I learned other things ... like you were a baseball player and your first and middle initial are RJ."

The mayor tensed, and his grip tightened on the glass. "And just want did you find?" His voice lowered, serious, almost menacing.

"Mayor, I'm sorry." She put down her glass. "When I took Aunt Gina's valuables to the bank safety deposit box, I discovered something I know she must have treasured."

"My letters ..."

Ashton shook her head. "Letters? No. It was a

charm with an endearment and your initials. Then I found her diary. I didn't know if RJ was still alive or even in the area until James told me he thought you'd lettered in baseball. Mrs. Atwood's declaration that you were all friends with Aunt Gina solved that mystery for me."

"And the other mystery—the story people around town tell about the inn? Have you solved it yet? Maybe in the diaries?"

"The gems?" She straightened in her seat. "I don't believe that's anything more than a tall tale, but I'm still reading through my aunt's journals, taking them in, as if they're special secrets she planned to share with me but never got around to it."

The mayor stared out toward Aunt Gina's workshop. "Would you mind ...?" He nodded toward the building.

"No. I haven't taken the time I need to get it cleaned up, but I hope to use her workshop as a studio to display her unsold works. However, I don't think I'll be able to part with them." She stepped inside the house and grabbed her keys from the counter. Then she walked with the mayor to the workshop. He peered into the dirty window as she unlocked the door.

Then he stepped inside in front of her. For a long moment, he took slow strides past the masterfully designed pieces. The colored glass was used to create everything from an intricate carousel to a beautiful monarch butterfly. Many other pieces depicted flowers and some even Biblical scenes.

The mayor stopped in front of an elaborate piece that depicted a young boy and young girl holding hands at what appeared to be a flowing stream. He reached out and stroked his hand over the depiction of the girl. "She was an artist." He took a handkerchief from his pocket and rubbed it under his nose. "Did you take after her in that respect?"

She smiled and picked up the beautiful work. "Not at all." She held it out to him. "I'd like for you to have this."

The mayor hesitated. "Why would you hand me something so valuable."

"You seem to have cared very much for Aunt Gina. Please accept this …"

"This has nothing to do with the letters?"

"Mayor Fernsby, I don't know about any letters, but you seem to be very concerned about them. I would like to hear what's so important, though, if you're willing to tell me." She offered the stained-glass piece to him once again.

This time he took it from her. "Thank you. I'll treasure this always." He took another look around. "I'm so glad that you plan to give her work a place to shine."

Ashton waited for the mayor to step out of the work shed before she followed. He moved back to the chair where he'd been sitting.

She, again, sat beside him.

The mayor stared at the work shed they'd just left. "I loved your Aunt Gina very much."

"Then why didn't the two of you marry?"

"The sad reality is that I caved to my father's pressure to marry Martha Van Cleve, daughter of a prominent political family who lived in our county's seat. My father thought I should go into politics—perhaps running for governor someday. Martha's family name would've helped, and she would've made a good first lady, in his opinion." The mayor stiffened his shoulders. "Those were my father's goals, not mine."

Ashton swallowed the tears that threatened. How could he have done that to her dear aunt who loved him so? How could he succumb to the pressure?

The mayor turned to Ashton. "You can't think anything less of me than I think of myself for allowing my father to dictate my future. I hurt two women, not just one. I've suffered a thousand times over through the years. I tried to make my marriage to Martha work, but I could never forget Gina. Then about fifteen years ago, I couldn't bear it any longer." He lifted his hand. "I never cheated physically on my wife. I couldn't do that do her, and I didn't want to cast shame on Gina either." He shook his head and looked down at his hands. "I minored in journalism in college. I speak better on paper, so I began to write her letters." He gulped. "She wrote me back. Through the medium of the written word, we relived all our years together. We shared our joys, our griefs, our blessings. I only saw her once during that time. An accidental meeting on the beach."

Ashton scooted to the edge of her seat. "What happened?"

"I did what I'd longed to do for years. Hold her. We said nothing but stood in each other's embrace for what seemed like hours. I never kissed her, but later, she smiled and walked away, her bare feet leaving prints in the sand. She told me in her next letter that it was the hardest thing she'd ever done. She'd been tempted to invite me to the inn, to be together, but she said her faith in God didn't allow it."

Ashton could feel the pain of having that last

embrace. "Mayor," she whispered, "what has you so worried about the letters? Gina's gone now. She kept your secret. I never knew about you, and I would never share her diary with anyone. James knows because I shared her love for RJ, and he helped me solve that mystery. James isn't going to betray my aunt or you."

He turned to look at her. "I know. As long as she was alive, I knew she would keep the letters, the evidence of our relationship, to herself. But after she died and you took over the inn—I'm sorry Ashton—if you were to make them public, my career as a politician would be over. I'd lose the respect of the town. They'd never understand the love I shared with your aunt— absolutely platonic but overwhelming in its depth." He held out the stained-glass. "These aren't children." He sat it on his lap and ran his hand over the young boy and girl. They're teenagers. I'd like to think that as she created this beautiful work of art, she thought of our love and the waters as something we just couldn't cross."

Never had a mixture of emotions torn at her like this. Anger, because he'd chosen his career over her aunt, and sorrow that Roy Fernsby and Gina had never consummated their love in matrimony. "Mayor, are you placing the roses on Aunt Gina's grave?"

"Yes, usually once a week. I ordered them online because everyone in Cranberry Cove knew Gina's penchant for yellow roses. They represent friendship, you know. In a way, it's a reminder to me that I'd allowed my father's ambitions to end that friendship with Gina. Yet, the love we had for each other never died. I deliver them under the protection of night."

Ashton bit her lip. The mayor's confession that he

knew what he'd done, softened her heart toward him. "Mrs. Atwood seems to know."

"She meant nothing by what she said. We relive old times quite often. She didn't know that Gina and I had seen each other one last time. To her, it's all ancient history, nothing to be hidden." The mayor offered her one of his warm smiles. They must have melted Aunt Gina's heart every time. "Have you found those letters?"

"I have not," she said. "I'm not even sure she kept them. I'd expect them to be with her diaries and her yearbooks, but they weren't there. Maybe she knew what they could do for your career, and maybe she destroyed them, allowing you to continue to choose it over her." She shook her head. That hadn't been a nice thing to say. "Mayor, I'm sorry. I respect the fact that you didn't leave your wife. Many men would 've done that. What I have trouble with is that you married her in the first place."

"Ashton, that's been the burden of my heart all these many years. I don't expect for you to have any respect for me at all. I hurt your aunt. I will not make demands of you, but I will appeal to you. Those letters are very, very private. Yes, your aunt's property belongs to you, but if she didn't do away with them and should you run across them, I would appreciate knowing."

Gina stood and took the glass from the mayor. "If I find them, I will let you know, and you can be sure that I would never invade your privacy. I know from her diary that my aunt loved you. Her leaving you on that beach is even more proof to me how much she must have cared for you. Seems she could have so easily had what she'd lost so long ago, but she understood that it would never end well if you cheated on your wife. I understand her momentary weakness in giving in and embracing you. That must've been the desire of her life. For her to walk away after that, well, she may have done it because of her relationship with God, but she also did it for your relationship with the woman to whom you were married. The thought of her loving you until her dying day makes me sad for her—and for you, Mayor Fernsby."

The mayor nodded and walked the way he had come. In his arms, he clutched the stained-glass piece to his chest. His head lowered, she realized, the mayor was crying.

James turned onto Main, passing Cove Community Church on the right. The sight of the steeple with the cross soaring twenty feet into the air tugged at his heart. The cross drew him in, reminding him he hadn't gone to services in months. The fellowship, the pastor's message—did he dare admit he missed church, that he needed the connection like a thirsty traveler coming upon an oasis.

Main changed to Rose Garden Lane as he drove to his cabin to change clothes. Drumming his fingers on the steering wheel didn't get him there any faster. As he'd predicted, working for Ashton after hours was a godsend—as if instead of a grave, a garden characterized his life. A literal garden.

In work boots and jeans, James parked in his usual spot at the inn and set out for the backyard.

Ashton reclined in a lawn chair on the deck. "I've got some strawberry lemonade waiting for you."

He edged into the recliner next to her and took the frosty glass with the strawberry on the rim. "Thanks. What jobs do you have for me today?"

She smiled and tapped his glass with her own. "First on the list is for me to tell you a story I learned about the inn and to tell you about the mayor's visit."

"Well, that has my attention."

As Ashton told him about the mayor's visit and the letters and then about the bride waiting for her groom for years, James thought about the depth of a love that endured without touch.

He had never truly loved Bethany. If only he'd discovered that before they had married. Bethany might still be alive, might be married to someone who truly cared for her. He wouldn't have had Sammy, and that thought cut him like a knife slipping into butter, but his little boy was lost to him anyway.

"James, are you okay?"

James nodded. "What will you do with the letters if you find them? You said you'd tell the mayor, but will you keep them."

Ashton shrugged. "If I ever find them, I'll decide then. I wanted the mayor to know they'll be safe with me if found. I would never betray my aunt by sharing them with anyone."

"I think Gina would be proud of you. She obviously loved him if she let him back into her life knowing they'd never be together. A sacrificial love like that is something few people get outside of the Lord." He left her to start his work.

She went back into the house.

He stopped and looked to the doorway she'd just entered. He'd failed miserably in his first attempt, but would he get a second chance to show Ashton that kind of love?

Sunday night, Ashton sat up in bed. Had she dreamed she'd heard a crash. No. The noise came from outside her apartment in the hall. And now, the scurrying of feet alerted her that someone may have been trying to sneak in her room. She slowly slipped her hand into the top drawer of the nightstand, her pulse pounding in her ears. She grasped the Smith and Wesson she'd retrieved from the pawn shop after the required waiting period, and with it in one hand and the flashlight in the other, she crept out of bed.

This couldn't be happening again. Though courage threatened to abandon her, she had to put a stop to the nightly visits.

In the hall not more than ten feet from her quarters, the decorative table rested on its side, and the door to the closet she'd planned to clean out tomorrow stood open.

She tiptoed to assure that the Claxtons' light wasn't on. She crept up the stairs and stared at the base of their door. Strange that they'd heard the water splash the last time an intruder came near, but they slept through the tumbling of a table.

Sneaking back down the stairs, she headed to the back door, her heart hammering, and she cocked the trigger. Out on the deck, she let the beam of the flashlight become a beacon in her search for anyone who could've been in the home.

A cloud partially covering the moon floated away, giving her a better view. A motor revved off in the distance—a motorcycle. The sound grew more pronounced, and Ashton turned off her flashlight as a single light wove its way through the darkness of the woods beyond the house.

That couldn't be a coincidence.

She shuddered and hurried inside. Were people actually this desperate to find gemstones that had never been proven anything more than a legend?

THE INN AT CRANBERRY COVE

Chapter Seventeen

Monday morning, James worked with his tie to form a knot. Taking a new client to lunch at the Bayside Restaurant required he dress up.

His phone rang. Ashton's name appeared on the screen. "Good morning."

"James, do you have a second?" A hint of panic laced her voice.

"Yeah, sure. What's going on?"

"Last night there was another disturbance."

He balled his fists. "What happened?"

"Around midnight, I heard a crash. Right outside my bedroom door. I was petrified. I grabbed my gun and left my room. A table in the hall had been knocked over, and before you ask, no. Maxwell was in my room with me."

James's hands grew cold. "Did it awaken your guests?"

"No. They apparently slept through it." She huffed. "I planned to ask them at breakfast, but they'd left. They've made a habit of letting me know when they won't be staying for breakfast, and I've made it a habit of asking them if I should prepare dinner."

"Ashton, are you worried about them?"

Ashton didn't speak for a long second, and James was sure she was gathering her thoughts. "I've had some doubts about them. At first, when they didn't hear the noise last night, I wondered how they could've been awakened by the lesser noise the night I called the police."

"What eased your concern last night?"

"A motorcycle. I went to the deck, and a motorcycle started. At first, I thought maybe a neighbor had a guest who was leaving late."

"But…?" Dread filled him.

"Their guests wouldn't be driving through the woods behind the inn."

James closed his eyes. "All right. Your guests don't seem to be of any help or safety, but their staying at the inn gives me the opportunity to check in as well, at least for the night."

"I can't ask you to do that."

"You're not asking. I'm volunteering. Besides, breakfast and your company will be my reward."

James parked his car in front of the inn beside Ashton. She'd called to tell him she'd have dinner ready so that they could eat before he did his evening yardwork. He reached in the backseat for his duffle, knocked, and entered the inn.

"Hope you like shrimp stir-fry." Ashton came from the kitchen.

"I love shrimp stir-fry. You said you were making

Caesar salad and strawberry pie, too?" He sat his duffle in a small chair that adorned the foyer. "And why can't I check in?" He followed Ashton to the kitchen.

Maxwell curled around his leg. "I think your cat likes me."

"He's probably hoping you have a treat in your pocket." Ashton set about preparing the meal.

"Sorry, buddy. All I have is a mint and a piece of gum. I don't think you'd go for these. Next time, I'll have some kitty catnip on me." He turned his attention to Ashton. "Is there anything I can do? Set the table? Pour the drinks?"

"I have this in hand. You've been working all day." Ashton hunted in the refrigerator and retrieved lettuce, a package of bleu cheese, and a bottle of dressing. She pointed to a door on the other side of the table. "But you can look in the pantry for a package of croutons. I think I have about everything else. " She glanced at his duffle bag. "I'm afraid I can't allow you to stay because my guests won't be joining us. I telephoned them to see if they planned to eat out for dinner. I was happy to tell them you were joining us, but they informed me they'd forgotten to mention they wouldn't be back for a few days. They're traveling around, and they thought it would be better to get rooms wherever they were for the night."

James understood her reluctance to house him, but what would she do if a single man made a reservation?

"James, you live close by. Mrs. Babbage is a very nice woman, but she might realize that you stayed here overnight, misread it, and out of habit, say something. You can understand, right?"

Yes, he did. "You are a very wise woman. With or

without Mrs. Babbage, I wouldn't want the rumors to destroy your reputation." He wouldn't say so, nor would he make a big deal out of their departure, but something wasn't sitting well with him about this couple. For one, he had yet to even see their car parked outside, not while driving by or while he worked here at the inn. James opened the door and walked into the large space. Can goods, bottles of catsup, mayo, mustard, and boxes of pasta filled the shelves. He reached to the highest shelf and grasped a bag. "Here you go." He set the bread cubes on the counter. "They've been here a while, and I have never met them. As much as I'm around, that seems strange."

Ashton stopped what she was doing and stared at him. "You do believe me that they're here, right? You don't think I've made them up?"

He laughed. "Never occurred to me."

"Because I can show you their room. I don't like going inside for anything but to clean it and give them fresh towels, but they've made themselves at home. I cleaned today. You can see."

"Ashton." He stilled her with a touch on her hand. "That you made up your guests never entered my mind. That I haven't seen them, though, you have to admit, does seem strange. I'm here almost every evening and all day on Saturdays."

She nodded. "They're always out until late, and on Saturdays, they make longer treks."

"Then they must really be traveling to stay gone so long."

Ashton nodded and continued to work at the kitchen counter. Being with her, preparing dinner, playing with the cat—he enjoyed her companionship.

But it wasn't fair—to her. His stomach twisted into a gnarl. She knew nothing about his failed marriage. She only felt sorry for him. He didn't deserve her pity. If they were to have a life together someday, she needed to know what happened the night before Bethany died. Maybe telling her would lift some of his heavy remorse.

Ashton washed the shrimp in the wide farmhouse sink and added them to hot oil in a cast-iron skillet. She measured out a half cup of almonds. "What are you thinking about? You're miles away."

He swallowed the apprehension before opening his mouth—to tell her a half-truth. "Just how blessed I am to be here with you. Getting ready for a delicious dinner."

She faced him, a frown on her face. "From how you're fidgeting, I'd say there's more."

"I… " The words lodged in his throat. He huffed. He couldn't tell her that the night before Bethany died, they'd argued. He'd yelled at her and pushed her onto the bed then spent the night at the inn. He even lied to Gina and said Bethany was having a ladies' card party. That he wanted to get out of her way.

A thousand times that night, he'd relived the appalling moment when he'd witnessed her flat on her back gaping up at him from the bed. Her mouth hung open in an incredulous stare as if she couldn't fathom what had happened.

Nor could he. Never before in his life had he raised a hand to a woman.

He'd pulled out his phone another thousand times to call her, but pride had gotten in the way.

The next day he went to work. He never saw her

alive again.

James gulped then spoke the only truthful words he could. "I… er, I'm allergic to almonds."

"What?" she laughed and gripped his arm. "You crazy guy. I thought it was something dire."

"I itch all over when I eat them." Heat worked its way up his cheeks. Would he ever find the courage to tell him the truth?

Aston poured the almonds back into the bag. "No problem. I'll save these for another time." She hummed a tune as she stirred the pasta and sautéed the shrimp in melted butter.

The urge to fold her in his arms almost overcame him. Yet he didn't deserve her—not until she knew—not until she had the choice to continue their relationship based upon knowing all about his past. "Maxwell took off. I guess he gave up on a treat. Let me help."

"Okay, I'll relent. Can you prepare the strawberries for the pie? I set the box in the fridge." She tiptoed to give him a peck on the cheek then whistled some song, all earlier tension gone.

He found the berries and washed them in the colander. "I haven't seen you this relaxed since I first met you."

"Unless someone decides to make a midnight visit, I'll sleep well."

He hoped no one came around … for Ashton's sake.

Chapter Eighteen

James looked up at the tap on his office door. "Hey, Dad."

"Son, your mother wants to meet us at the Wharf for lunch. She's waiting."

She never asked to meet them both for lunch.

James clicked off his computer and studied Dad's face. Guess he must've been a poker player in the day. He revealed no clue as to what Mom wanted. No sense in asking, either. Dad would only offer some kind of a meaningless comment. "You never know what your mom's up to."

Leslie looked up from her computer as they walked out the door.

"Be back in a couple of hours." James nodded.

After they walked the three blocks to the elegant seafood restaurant, James held the door for his dad. From a table by the window with a view of the bay, Mom waved.

Her hand flashed her long red fingernails. She patted the chair adjacent to hers. "Sit here, James. It's not every day I get to eat lunch with my son."

James offered a smile that he hoped said he was

glad as well. After ordering iced tea, he looked at Mom. "What's keeping you busy these days?"

Mom brushed a strand of brown hair from her cheek. Her gray eyes carried a spark. Something was up. "Just my clubs and volunteering."

A waiter delivered a steaming plate of some kind of seafood to the table next to them. The aroma of garlic, tomatoes, and cilantro whetted his appetite.

After their entrees of salmon filets, buttered scallops, and seafood risotto, Mom took a sip of her peppermint mocha. She focused on him. "Son, I was delighted to see that you're beginning to get out with friends. Ashton Price seems like a nice girl. Her aunt was a sweet woman."

"Marie, this isn't the best time…" Dad dabbed his mouth with his napkin.

James raised his hand. "No, it's okay, Dad." He knew Mom would eventually reveal her thoughts—her motives for the lunch today. He peered at her. "You're right. Ashton is merely a friend. She needs temporary help with the inn."

Mom lifted her brows. "I'm glad to hear it. I noticed, though, that you seemed uncomfortable with introducing her to us. Son, we lost so much, but you don't have to be worried about us if you're ready to move forward."

Dad lifted his brows. "Marie, James just said he's helping out at the inn. The way you're talking, you'd think they were romantically involved."

Mom lifted her chin and gave James a knowing smile. "Just so our son knows that we support him with his work at the inn."

James laughed. "Okay, Mom. I get your point.

After Ashton Price, you'll be the first to know if I decide to move on."

The sunrays bouncing off the broad leaf trees beside the road were brighter this morning as Ashton drove into town. She smiled. She hadn't realized how much a good night's sleep would help.

She rolled down the window, the fresh morning air elevating her spirits. With only the soaring Douglas fir to listen, she raised her voice. "I'm going to officially open the inn."

With the Claxtons away, she'd done some thinking. The time was right.

She wiggled the fingers of her right hand as she gripped the steering wheel with her left. The new website she'd spent three hours on this afternoon challenged her like no other she'd worked up. Especially the page where guests could make reservations and find out more information about the inn.

"Aunt Gina, your inn is coming to life once more," she announced to the trees again.

She eyed her grocery list in the passenger seat—cleaning supplies, coffee, hard mints. After ten minutes she drove up to Hometown Grocery.

The place was busy. Ashton parked in a space farthest from the door and stepped out.

"Excuse me." A well-dressed woman with short brown hair walked at a brisk pace toward Ashton. "Mrs. Atwood."

"Call me Marie." The woman held out a well-manicured hand.

"Nice to meet you again." Ashton shook the woman's hand.

"James rushed away when he last met, and we didn't truly get to meet."

Ashton could ask James's mother so many questions, but she wouldn't do that to him.

"James hasn't said, but I believe you have become quite important to him."

Ashton caught her breath. Had Marie Atwood read her son correctly? The woman seemed almost hopeful, but Ashton couldn't speak for James. "We've become friends. James has graciously offered to keep up the grounds until I can find someone else."

Marie placed her hand on Ashton's shoulder. "Honey, as you are probably aware, James has suffered a great deal of trauma in the last months."

"He told me about the tragic death of his wife and son, yes."

"When I saw him with you after the parade, I realized that James may be starting to leave the grief behind. I have to admit that when he told me he was working for Gina at the inn, I was concerned that he was doing as he has always done and burying his grief with toil. James hides from unpleasant truths by working. Then I talked to Gina, and she explained that her offer had at least gotten him out of the office at quitting time and during the weekends. I'll always be thankful for that."

Ashton didn't know how to answer, so she remained quiet.

"You've been good for my son, too. And I wanted

to say thank you." The woman's eyes filled with tears. "Oh goodness. Look at me." She dug in her purse and pulled out a tissue. "That's all I wanted to say, but I do hope to see you again."

"I hope so, too," Ashton managed.

"Well, I'll let you get to your shopping. Let me know when you open the inn. I volunteer at the Chamber and for other organizations. I'll definitely help you to promote, and if you plan to serve brunch or other meals to non-guests, I'll keep you busy with my groups and friends."

"That's why I'm here today. I have had a couple staying at the inn. Aunt Gina failed to cancel their reservation, but the Claxtons have gone for a bit, and I think I'm ready to begin to take other reservations. I may open for other events slowly, as I gain experience."

"Claxtons," Marie said the name as if she recognized it.

"Do you know them? I get the idea they may have lived here before. Mr. Claxton retired, and they ventured back from California for a visit."

Was that tension that fell from Marie's shoulders? "Goodness. I thought it might be someone I know, but they were never from here. They came for a bit many years ago, but they moved to Idaho. I don't know where they've been. I haven't thought of them in years."

Ashton took a breath she hadn't realized until that moment that she'd been holding. Her suspicions of the couple were unfounded after all. For a moment, she envisioned herself putting the Claxtons' possessions on the front porch and calling to tell them they had been evicted."

But Oggie would probably demand a refund for the rest of their extended stay, and Ashton couldn't have afforded it. She had yet to find their deposit, and it'd be her word against theirs.

"You have a nice day, dear." Mrs. Atwood waved as she stepped away.

Ashton smiled.

Another relief fell over her. She didn't have to worry about making friends with James's mother should James think of Ashton as more than a friend.

Marie Atwood seemed to be rooting for their friendship to develop into something more.

Chapter Nineteen

Ashton pulled the covers down and settled into her bed, Aunt Gina's diary in her lap. She couldn't concentrate. Aunt Gina's romance was overshadowed by the thought that Mrs. Atwood thought James might have romantic intentions toward Ashton.

After fifteen minutes, she set Aunt Gina's journal on top of the nightstand, switched off the lamp, and relaxed into the comfy pillow she'd scented with lavender. Maxwell's rhythmic purring quieted her, easing the cares of the day. She'd just about drifted to sleep.

Crash! Ashton bolted up in bed, her heart hammering.

Maxwell howled and shot under the bed.

A chill raced her spine. She hadn't merely dreamed the sound. Her cat had heard the crash as well.

Ashton slowly extended her hand toward the nightstand's top drawer. She wrapped her fingers around the gun's handle and crept out of the bed. She'd thought surely the person trying to invade her home had given up by now. At the door of her apartment, she froze.

She had to make a decision. Flight or fight, and she chose to fight. She opened the apartment door and gripped her handgun tighter. A moonlit haze illuminated the hall as she tiptoed past the decorative table in the entry to the living room.

She gasped and cocked the gun. On the floor next to the cabinet that housed Aunt Gina's book collection and keepsakes, the Blue Willow bowl lay shattered.

Blood buzzed in her ears as the truth settled in. Someone had invaded her home once again. The peace she thought she'd gained evaporated in one ruthless moment. She crept to the kitchen and then into the chapel. No one.

Her raw nerves made her shiver. What about upstairs? No, she couldn't explore the guestrooms on the second floor—or the first. Her fight mode threatened to abandon her.

She ran to her apartment, shut and locked the door, and grabbed for her cell phone. She was a prisoner within a jail cell of fear.

After three rings, James answered, his voice groggy. "Ashton, what is it?"

"James." She wavered. "Can you come over?"

"I'm on my way." A shuffling sound. "What happened?"

"Someone got inside again."

"Call 9-1-1 and wait inside by the front entrance. Shoot to kill if anyone approaches from inside the inn. I'll be there in a few." The sound of a motor carried over the line.

James was on his way.

"Please hurry." Her hands shaking, she made the call to the police. They'd be there in twenty minutes, the dispatcher said. Thankfully, James would be sooner.

Ashton wished she'd grabbed her flashlight. She held her breath and listened for sound. An eerie silence permeated the air around her. In two minutes, a soft knock sounded at her front door. "Ashton, it's me," James whispered.

She flung the door open then relented to the comfort of his strong arms, savoring the warm pressure from his hands on her back. She allowed herself to depend on his strength for a moment then moved away, brushing her unruly hair from her eyes.

James, in a t-shirt and exercise joggers, pulled a gun from under the elastic waist band. "Is the intruder still in the house?"

She switched on the hall lights. "I don't think so, but I only searched the living room, chapel, and kitchen."

"Did you call the police?"

"Yes." Her teeth chattered though it wasn't cold in the inn.

"All right. Stay here. I'll search the guest rooms upstairs."

"Okay. The light switch is on the wall."

He looked toward the spiral staircase and rotated to her, gripping her hand. "It's okay, Ashton. I'm here for you."

Ashton smiled weakly and leaned against the door's inside frame.

Within fifteen minutes, someone knocked at the entrance. "Ma'am, it's the police."

She inched open the door and peeked out. Two different officers from the last time she'd called stood on the porch.

"Dispatch said there's an intruder in your home."

"A crash woke me. Someone was in the living area. I found a broken vase on the floor." She motioned for them to follow.

"Are you here alone, ma'am." The second cop pulled out his gun. "I hear footsteps upstairs."

"That's my friend. I called him first, and he's searching the inn as well."

The second cop gripped his gun. "Okay, but I'm going up there to check, just in case."

"He has a gun on him, too." Ashton told the advancing officer as she led the first officer to the broken vase.

He fingered the gun on his belt and bent over to examine the broken glass.

A cool breeze she hadn't notice before blew through the living room.

"The point of entry." The officer walked toward the wall with the deck beyond. "Did you leave the window up? Looks like someone removed the screen."

"Oh, no." She tapped her forehead. "Yesterday afternoon, I opened it to get a breeze flowing and forgot to close it." Never again would she make that mistake.

She swallowed the desperation that was trying to overwhelm her. For the first time since she'd taken possession of the inn, she wanted to leave—to forget her dreams of running the place. To flee to anywhere but here. Her fingers were cold—and numb.

After searching the kitchen and chapel, the policeman turned to Ashton. "I'm going to check the guest rooms on this floor."

The kitchen chair supported her exhausted body. The cops and James were here, so she was safe for the moment. She rubbed her arms in an attempt to comfort herself. Her face warmed as she realized she was barefoot and wore only her pajamas. She rose and peered out the back door toward the side yard.

She held the breath inside her lungs. Near Mrs. Babbage's property, a light bobbed up and down then disappeared. Her nerves coiled so tightly she figured she might have a breakdown. Turning around, she paced to the hallway. What was the source of the light? Could Mrs. Babbage be in danger?

After what seemed like two hours, James returned with the second officer.

The policeman slipped his gun in his belt. "All clear upstairs. Good thing you told me about this guy, or I might've shot him." He winked.

A smile played at the corners of James's mouth. "If this weren't a serious situation, I might've laughed." He looked up as the first cop who returned to the kitchen.

"All clear down here. Tony, let's do a search outside." He pointed toward the window in the living area. "Someone removed the screen."

Ashton raked a hand through her messy hair. "I think I saw a beam from a flashlight over in that direction a few minutes ago." She pointed toward Mrs. Babbage's property. "She's an elderly woman who lives alone."

"All right. We'll check."

James took a few steps toward her after the officers left by the backdoor. He pushed a strand of hair from her face. "I'm staying the rest of the night—and maybe a few more until we discover who's behind this. I won't take no for an answer. " He snickered. "Your argument was well taken before, but I think we left one idea out of the equation. If Mrs. Babbage knows what is going on and the reason I'm staying and that I'm staying in a separate room, that could work in our favor. If this is someone from town, they'll get the message that you're on defense."

Ashton nodded and dabbed at the moisture in her eye that she hoped James wouldn't see. At this point, she didn't care what Mrs. Babbage would assume. Unless she wanted to abandon the inn and Aunt Gina's dream, she welcomed the protection.

After twenty more minutes, the cops stepped inside from the backyard. The first returned a flashlight to his belt. "We tested the area around the screen for fingerprints, but whoever was here must've worn gloves. No noticeable footprints. I doubt we'll find anything from the broken vase. We'll make a report on the incident and ask the captain to assign more patrol cars to the area."

"Thank you, officers. I hope whoever was here will get discouraged and not come back."

"We can always hope." The first officer scratched his head. "Do you have any idea why someone would break in or what they might be looking for?"

Ashton paused as she stared straight ahead. "My aunt, the prior owner, told me that she had trouble with guests over the years. They showed up with an ulterior motive of finding the gems that legend has it are hidden in the house. After her death, the neighbor said she'd see lights in the house. I believe someone is desperate enough to search while I'm here."

"What some people won't do if they hear about a dollar or two." One of the officers shook his head. "Okay. Don't hesitate to call any time." The two men left by the front door.

She turned to James sitting at the kitchen table. "One thing I can be sure of. It wasn't a ghost. Ghosts don't remove screens to get in. And I finally have tangible evidence that what I'm experiencing is actually happening."

"Whoever entered your home had flesh and bones." James hmphed. "I honestly hoped the intrusions were over, but now... Ashton, I think you used the correct word. Someone is desperate for something that probably doesn't exist. Desperate people can be dangerous.""

Ashton dressed quickly and glanced out her bedroom window. James's car was still parked in the same spot where he'd driven it to last night. No sound of anyone stirring so he was likely still asleep in the guestroom. She'd hurry to the kitchen to make coffee.

She rolled her eyes. Surprising, Mrs. Babbage hadn't knocked on her door asking about the police and her overnight guest. Ashton sighed. Yet, James was right. Mrs. Babbage wasn't a fabricator of gossip. She simply repeated it. That could be helpful in keeping hers—and James's—reputations in good repute while, at the same time, alerting any would-be burglar that they were keeping watch. "I pray, Lord, for Your protection."

The Lord. She couldn't deny she needed Him. Aunt Gina had always said she wanted the inn to be a place where guests could rest, recuperate from the pressures of life, and reconnect with God. Ashton needed a new connection with her Savior, too. Maxwell bounded out of the room when she opened her apartment door.

In the kitchen, James sat at the kitchen table, a cup of steaming coffee in front of him. "I hope you don't mind. I made myself at home and notified work I'd be a little late."

"I felt so much better knowing you were here. How was your guest room?"

"I used the complementary toothbrush and paste by the bathroom sink."

"Great. I guess that makes you my third unofficial guest."

"I slept well. No ghosts up on the second floor." His eyes twinkled with his smile.

Ashton poured a cup of coffee and edged down across from him.

"I read a Biblical teaching about the supernatural," James said. "There are spirits from the underworld, but they certainly aren't our dead relatives or any other person who once lived on the earth."

"You're right. I haven't talked about this lately, but I believe in the Lord and His word." She peered at him. "I strayed from church when I had problems with my job, and I'm not happy about my delay in returning to worship. I need to again—and to fellowship with others."

His face lit. "I was thinking the same. I'll go with you."

She studied the man across the table from her. A light stubble covered his cheeks. When he looked at her, his soft blue eyes spoke of compassion and hope. As if life with him would make sense. His long, patrician nose and well-shaped lips always hinting of a smile set her heart pattering harder.

"Ashton?" He reached for her hand.

She glanced down at her coffee cup, her face warm. "I'm sorry. I suppose I was staring."

"What's on your mind?"

"I ran into your mother the other day at the grocery. She said—"

James sat up straight, a frown on his forehead. "My mother?"

"She seemed to think we are… you know, growing into an item. I tried to tell her you were merely a friend and helped me with the yard."

"I'm sorry if she overstepped."

"No, she was really very nice. She was grateful for Aunt Gina for getting you out of the office. She did say you tend to turn to work to avoid things."

James straightened. "She said that? Did she happen to tell you the things I avoid, too?" He stood and moved toward the coffeepot.

"James, she intimated that you seem to be coming out of a period of grief. She's happy to see it."

He took a drink of coffee and put down his cup. "My mother can be overly dramatic. I work because I have a lot to do."

Ashton studied her own cup, now almost empty. "I worked for a man that always had a lot to do."

"The guy who fired you over the word of another would-be lover?"

She nodded but didn't dare look at him. Something in his tone said that he was agitated at his mother. She hated that she'd made that happen.

James sat down again. "Ashton." Her name fell

softly from his lips. "I never cheated on my wife. When I was at work, I was at work. My mother didn't lie to you when she said I use my job to avoid things. I do. I'm hoping to change that."

"She didn't say this, so don't think she conveyed it in anyway, but are you using the work here at the inn as an avoidance of anything or anyone?"

He gave a soft smile. "In some ways, I believe I am, but not as much as I used to. Lately, I've been rushing home from work and reporting to duty because of the pretty innkeeper."

James reached for her hand. "Ashton, I—"

The house phone sitting on her computer desk rang. "Excuse me a moment." She rose from the seat, picked up the handset, and strolled out to the deck.

After five minutes, she returned. "One of Aunt Gina's previous customers. She wanted to know when I was opening." She squealed. "I've got my first official reservation."

A knock sounded on the back door. "Yoo hoo, Ashton."

Ashton smiled. "First order of business, getting Mrs. Babbage to spread the word to keep these idiots from trying to search the inn during the night."

"I'll do whatever I can." James stood. Mrs. Babbage had saved him from sharing with Ashton the circumstances surrounding his dead wife.

Chapter Twenty

The sun drew closer to the western horizon as James studied the crumbled segment of brick at the base of the old fountain. Ashton should probably consider replacing the entire thing and installing a new solar pump. Using a chisel, he removed the fragmented piece and turned it over in his hand. Since only one side had begun to decompose, he filled the hole in the base with mortar, turned the brick the other way, and slipped it in place. Brushing the dirt off his hands, he rose.

"Hey, James. Join me for chicken sandwiches and apple slices." Ashton's yellow sundress billowed with the slight breeze.

All weekend, he'd thought of nothing else. Ashton, the inn, the invasions—and telling her about the past. If only Mom hadn't tried to play matchmaker. He couldn't hope to be more than friends with so much standing between him and Ashton.

He stomped the dirt off his boots before he stepped onto the deck. "After eight hours at the office, I'm starved. Thanks. I take it your guests haven't returned."

Ashton set a tray on the side table between two lounge chairs. "No. I haven't heard from them. I should call to make sure they're okay, but I'm only their innkeeper. I don't want to be intrusive. Sit. I'll get us some lemonade." She turned toward the back door.

When she returned, her dark hair shone in the setting sun that cast a warm glow to her skin as well. He'd almost kissed her the day at the beach. Why not now? Yes, he had to admit. He was falling for her. He wanted to be there for her. To help her through this time. He could picture them as a family, raising children together.

He lightly touched her arm and drew her to him.

She relaxed in his arms for a moment then moved away. "Maybe we'd better eat now."

Ashton wanted to remain in James's arms forever. But if his mother was right, and if James worked to keep from dealing with his issues, by the very nature of his continual work ethic, grief still lingered, or something—or someone—had his attention.

While she was beginning to want more than a friendship, Ashton doubted it could work now.

She sat and passed him a plate of the lunch she'd prepared.

Though she loved his arms around her and the evergreen scent of his aftershave, maybe he shouldn't continue working at the inn. "Maybe you should take some time and relax, give some thoughts to what's happened to you. I'm sure your loss has been difficult."

James pressed his lips together then shook his head. "Ashton, this is my way of moving on. Now, if you said you didn't want me around for another reason, I won't force my help upon you."

Ashton blew out a ribbon of air. "I love what you do around here but have you really had time to heal?"

He grabbed both her hands. "Please don't send me away. The inn and the yard mean so much." He hung his head. "But there is something I haven't told you. Just not yet."

Ashton couldn't take her eyes from him. Behind his handsome face and inside his head, a secret dwelled. Though she hoped James would allow her to carry part of the burden, she'd have to wait until he was ready.

Doubt began to niggle her. James had already shared the loss of his wife and son. Was there another part of his life he didn't want to talk about? Would she ever understand what bothered him? She couldn't have a life with him otherwise.

THE INN AT CRANBERRY COVE

Chapter Twenty-one

The next day at work, James leaned back in his chair and closed his eyes. Strange, the several times he had to pass Robert's office, he saw his cousin on the phone. In each incident, he heard Robert speak the name of one of his relatives on his mother's side—someone James remembered as a troublemaker. Maybe Robert got his personality from his mother's family. James smiled but then stopped. Robert's mother was a sweet woman. She couldn't help what others in her family did.

He opened his eyes and glanced at the wall clock. Time for lunch, but today he'd eat in the office. He needed time to think—to think about Ashton and who could possibly be showing up in the middle of the night.

He slipped the bologna sandwich from the paper bag he'd retrieved from the employee refrigerator and took a bite. After a few nights of absolutely nothing occurring, they gambled that Mrs. Babbage had unintentionally done her job, spread the rumors that someone was on guard, and Ashton was safe. He was beginning to miss his stay in the inn's guest room.

Ashton's chicken sandwiches were more appealing than the one he'd made in his own kitchen this morning at six thirty when he slapped the ingredients on a piece of dry bread.

James munched a bite of the spicy meat. Mental note. Ask Ashton for her chicken salad recipe.

He scratched his head. An unknown individual believed gems existed at the inn. They wanted them desperately enough to break in at least twice since Ashton moved in.

He chewed another bite and stared at his computer. Maybe he should look at the inn's history. Ashton had researched, but maybe he could find something else. The establishment had existed since the mid-1800s. Maybe he'd turn up a clue.

He checked out a couple of sites about the history of Cranberry Cove. The cranberry business, as he well knew, started in the early 1800s but died down at the change of the century when the demand for the fruit came to an end. However, years later, Pacific Cranberry opened its doors, and the industry boomed all over the state.

He frowned. Interesting, but that didn't seem to have any bearing on the inn. He switched to another site. A banker had lived in the house during the gold rush, and that family's descendants had continued to live there until the home was sold to Gina. During the gold rush, almost three hundred thousand people streamed into California from other areas of the US. Cranberry Cove, Washington, had been a stop along the journey. James continued to search. A very old article in the society section of the newspaper caught his eye. He downloaded a pdf of the document and printed it out. Then he searched for another clue. Finding it, he printed it as well. Gina's legend had a basis for reality. Could the person who illegally entered the inn actually have this information as well? He'd have to share it with Ashton this afternoon.

With his head in his hands, he closed his eyes. "Lord, please show Ashton what to do."

Later in the afternoon, James rubbed his eyes. Working on potential new accounts for the last three hours had tired him. He needed a cup of coffee to perk up.

He turned down the hall and toward the back of the building to the employee's room. As he passed Robert's office, once again a phone conversation slowed his pace.

Leslie didn't look up from her cubicle as James took a few steps toward the open door. Okay, call him nosey, but he had to know if his cousin was up to something.

"I'll make sure. I'll let you know. Yes. It's important. If I'd been able to get my hands on it, I wouldn't need you, would I? You're lucky I cut you in on this." Robert was not happy. His tone was low but menacing."

James frowned and turned his ear toward the office door.

"I'm working on that as well. I'll get her to sell out. I want it. She'll be sorry if I don't get my way. No. Dad's tied my hands. I don't have anything to give to you. If you're out of money, you'll have to return, won't you? You'll have to make sure you're not seen."

What?

Another pause.

"When we get what we want, you won't have to worry about that any longer will you? Just do as I say. And be careful. James can't know what's going on. I'm working on Dad about the presidency, but to tell you the truth, something's going on with him. Yeah, James, I'm sure."

What was his cousin taking about? A sellout? But to whom? And James would make sure his cousin didn't control of the company. He'd rather have to sell it to someone who would keep the employees in their jobs. Robert would plunder everything and make it irredeemable.

Never mind confronting Robert. He'd deny what he said and accuse James of eavesdropping—which was the truth.

No. James would hold the knowledge close to his vest. Uncle Terrance, as Robert had indicated, was keeping Robert at a distance. James felt sorry for both his uncle and his cousin. James couldn't imagine going behind his own father's back. If his father lost trust in him, James would never forgive himself.

Robert had never been the type to care about family. Actually, he'd never cared about anyone but himself, and apparently, he was up to no good. James would need to keep an eye on him.

Chapter Twenty-two

James parked to the side of the inn and leaned his head on the seatback. He'd stewed on Robert's conversation with the caller and wondered if the calls he'd listened in on had been with the same individual. But what were they doing?

He spotted Ashton on the deck. Maybe he could talk to her about the problem. Or maybe not. He had to admit that the family's reputation was important. Was that the reason he didn't want to tell her about that fateful night.

At least he could be grateful she didn't order him not to return. Though he savored the tranquility of the plants and trees, now he realized it was more. He wanted to be near her. To help her discover who had invaded her home. He stepped out of the car and headed toward the deck.

"Hey, James. How was work?"

"It had its challenges." He breathed deeply of the warm scent of roses bordering the deck. "Better now that I'm here." He slipped into the chair next to her. "Before I get too comfortable, what do you have for me to do in the yard today? I was thinking about repairing more of the brick on the fountain."

She rubbed her hands together. "What would you say to a treasure hunt? I'd like to find those letters Mayor Fernsby wrote to Aunt Gina."

He chuckled. "I did a little research today." He reached into this back pocket and pulled out the folded copies he'd printed in his office.

"What did you learn?"

"That the basis for the myth is true."

"Well, I knew that," she teased. "Most myths might have a basis for truth. A person lives and dies in a home is the basis for a ghost story, but ghosts aren't real, as we've already discussed."

"But a banker during a gold rush with a daughter of marriageable age, adds credence to the legend." He unfolded the papers. "Then when you find an engagement notice for the couple …" He held out the article. She took it and read it. "And then you find out that she never married …"

"Her fiancé was from the east, was said to be from society, and they did plan to marry when he returned from California. You have to be kidding me."

"And then you find this proof that she never married …" He handed her the obituary he'd found for the poor woman. "That basis seems a lot more concrete, doesn't it?"

Ashton smiled the biggest smile she'd given him since they'd met. "Hmm. We should start in the attic? If we can't find the letters, maybe we'll unearth the gemstones."

He glanced toward the soaring peeked roof.

Ashton stared toward the Douglas fir on the back of the property. "I haven't gone up there yet."

"Okay, let's try the first two floors again." James

ran his finger over the chair's armrest. "Maybe a second set of eyes would help. What about the apartment? That seems the logical place. Have you checked there?"

"Yes, all the drawers and closets."

He stood. "Let's search again. I'll take the guest rooms, and you do the others on the first floor. And let's look for any secret hiding places where Gina may have hidden the letters or ones she may not have found while she lived here—where the gems could be hidden." He firmed his jaw.

Later, the sun had neared the horizon when James took the ornate, spiral staircase back to the first floor.

Ashton slid a box into the hall closet and closed the door. "Any luck?"

"No, I even checked under the beds. No letters. Should we search the attic?" He rubbed his neck. "Maybe she put them up there because she'd begun to believe writing letters to each other wasn't a good idea." He touched her arm to restrain her. "You don't think she destroyed them?"

Ashton smiled. "No. I did tell the mayor she might have, but I'm sure she didn't. I've learned from her journal how much she cared for the man. She would never have done that."

"Okay. You understand women better than I." He chuckled. "They mystify me most of the time."

She gave him a playful tap. "It's the same way we feel about guys, you know."

James rolled his eyes.

"Okay, let's explore the attic." She refastened the clip that swept her hair off her neck. "But I need for you to stay with me because dark, spider-infested places aren't my thing."

He laughed and waved his hand for them to go. "While I was up on the second floor, I spotted the staircase that leads to the attic. I looked around a bit. I didn't see even one spider."

Ashton strode by his side up the stairs from the first floor. They passed the guest room where he'd spent that infamous night before Bethany died. He averted his gaze and stopped at the attic stairs. "Ladies first."

"No, you go first." Ashton rubbed her arms. "And don't leave me."

He chuckled. "Nothing to be afraid of in an old attic."

"Yes, there is." She shivered. "Are there lights up here?"

James flipped the switch. An electric bulb bathed the area with light. "When was the inn wired for electricity? It's handy they added it to the attic as well though there is another source of light at one end—near the fireplace. It's a stained-glass window."

Ashton's footsteps sounded behind him. "I've taken that one for granted and barely look at it. It's visible above the chapel."

Rafters met at the ceiling, forming a V. "Looks like most of the wood could be the original. Amazing how these old buildings were so well constructed. But there had to have been repairs through the years."

Ashton walked beside him as they made their way along the center aisle.

To the west, the setting sun sent its final rays through the glasswork, painting the walls and floors in red, gold, blue, and green.

Ashton inhaled and grabbed his hand. "It's beautiful. Let's take a closer look. This was one of Aunt

Gina's first projects."

He enjoyed the warmth of her soft skin as they made their way toward the light. A lamb lay in the grass. Beyond the lamb a lion seemed not to be seeking it for prey, but guarding it from harm. "She really was amazing."

"I know. You've been working so hard, I haven't wanted to ask, but I'd like to clean up her workshop and make it a showcase for the inn's visitors to enjoy the work she didn't sell before she died."

"I will get to work on that soon. Your wish is my command." He laughed. "Let's give this place a thorough search. If we can't find the gems or the letters anywhere, we'll have to assume they aren't here."

The disappointment of not finding the letters or the gemstones had kept Ashton awake most of the night. The gems weren't really the issue. She liked the treasure hunt, but the absence of the letters bothered her. Mrs. Babbage had seen lights in the house before Ashton had been able to arrive. Someone had definitely been inside the house since her arrival. If they had stolen the letters, would they use them to blackmail the mayor.

That idea was what had left her sleepless, and right now, in the early morning, she needed a Starbucks.

She parked in municipal parking, got out of her car, and walked north. She trekked to the end of the street past Pacific Cranberry's business office then turned the corner. She could almost smell the aroma of a mocha latte laced with cinnamon sprinkles.

An eerie chill drifted down her neck. Something wasn't right. Maybe it was her imagination. Yet, she knew. Someone followed her. She turned to her left.

A tall, younger woman with stringy blond hair leaned against the stone wall in front of Pacific Cranberry. Her pants were slick and her shirt was grungy. A black motorcycle helmet was tucked under one arm. She stared at Ashton but quickly averted her gaze. Ashton quickened her pace as she passed town hall. Strange. When Ashton imagined an intruder, she'd thought it would be a man. A woman? And was this woman stalking her? If so, she didn't move to keep up.

Ashton increased her pace and scooted through Starbuck's front door. Inside, the familiar surroundings soothed her concern. She shook her head. Maybe she was getting paranoid.

Ashton stepped in line behind three customers. Besides a latté, she needed a bag of ground coffee. She glanced over her shoulder to the display shelf.

A shiver prickled her body as she peered beyond the case and out the window. Across the street, the same woman in the dark clothing stood in front of a health food store staring at her. Ashton moved up in line and out of her view.

"Hey, Ashton. Your usual?"

She turned to the barista. "Oh, yes, thanks, Gracie."

Gracie grinned and pulled a medium-sized paper cup off the stack.

Ashton lowered her voice and crooked her finger. "Can you do me a favor? Look out the window and tell me if you've ever seen that woman before." She pointed toward the shelf.

Gracie frowned then shrugged her shoulders.

"Sure."

Ashton grasped the barista's arm and nudged her nearer the window. "Look across the street."

Gracie lifted her eyebrows then took a few steps forward. "What's going on?"

Ashton stared over Gracie's shoulder and huffed. The woman was no longer there. "She's gone."

"Who's gone?"

"Don't think I'm crazy." Ashton clutched her forehead and shook her head. "Someone followed me here. At least I think they did. A woman. She was there a few minutes ago."

Gracie offered a weak smile and patted Ashton's back. "Come. Sit down. I think you've been working too hard. You need a latte."

Ashton trudged behind her to the bar. "Maybe I'm making too much of this. I've had some weird things going on lately."

"Or maybe you've been watching too many detective movies."

James parked in his usual spot at the inn and checked his watch. If he'd had his way, he would've arrived earlier, but Robert had quietly learned from billing, and then from Uncle Terrance, that his embezzlement days were over. He'd been ugly toward Leslie most of the day, and James was not surprised to have received some of his cousin's wrath.

Robert had calmed down when Dad and Uncle Terrance had entered his office. Dad told him later that

Robert was given an ultimatum to abide by the rules that all employees, including owners, lived by, or he could find another job.

Uncle Terrance had even admitted that it would be better if Robert quit. Leslie had been performing Robert's duties exceptionally well.

On the deck, Ashton paced from one end to the other. "Hey. Don't wear out the wood on the deck floor." His joke didn't bring a smile to her face.

She glanced up with a creased brow and lips pressed tightly in a line. She crept toward him. "James, someone was following me today."

He took the steps two at a time. "What happened? I pray you weren't assaulted."

"No," she said. "When I went into town, I walked to Starbucks. I saw a woman in front of your office just standing there. She carried a motorcycle helmet. She glanced at me then to the sky as if she didn't want me to know she'd stared. She wasn't a local, I'm sure."

"There are tourists this time of the year. Maybe she's a visitor to Cranberry Cove."

"No. Let me finish. I walked around the block to Starbucks. After I got in line, I glanced out the window. She was there again—across the street." She touched her throat. "I'm really getting scared."

James reached for her hand and held it tightly in his.

She swiped a hand over her eyes. "When Gracie went to look, the stalker had disappeared." Ashton raised her voice. "I know I saw her. I'm not going crazy."

With all his heart, James wanted to hold her, to protect her. He drew her into his arms and nuzzled her cheek then whispered. "Together we can figure this out."

She ran her hand down his shoulder. "Thank you for being here for me."

Chapter Twenty-three

Ashton leaned back in her rolling chair and gave her computer screen a sideways glance. Her plans for the breakfast and midafternoon hors d'oeuvre menus looked perfect. Now if she only had guests to enjoy them. Her first real reservation was a month out.

She'd heard from the Claxtons earlier in the day. They were returning soon, but they had been vague. She would no longer plan her time around them. They had a room to stay at night, and more and more, she was beginning to disbelieve their story about Aunt Gina and the reservations.

She stood and stretched her arms and shoulders. The fresh air outside called to her. Since July offered pleasant weather, she'd better soak up the sun. Fall would be here soon enough.

She stepped onto the wooden deck and glanced toward the window where the intruder had broken in the other night. Her deck, her gardens. How many times had someone invaded them uninvited?

She plopped into a yard chair and breathed in the aroma of honeysuckle. Whoever broke into the inn probably lived close by as the disturbances had persisted over several months now.

A shrill voice carried in the air.

Ashton jerked upright.

Mrs. Babbage—hollering at the deer again.

Ashton snapped her fingers. Mrs. Babbage was her greatest weapon of defense. She rose and paced toward the borderline between hers and Mrs. Babbage's properties.

Ashton strolled down the path to Aunt Gina's gravesite. Fresh yellow roses. Ashton had given the mayor permission to fill the container.

She knelt down in front of the headstone. "If only you were alive and could help James and me."

She closed her eyes and allowed the cool summer breeze to tickle her cheek then lift her hair from her neck. No matter what, she loved living in Cranberry Cove—if only she could get the inn open and underway.

As if the wind whispered in her ear, she perceived the words. *Trust in Me*. She shivered, not from fear but of something else—joy? If she didn't know better, she'd think the Lord had spoken to her. The same God Aunt Gina had introduced her to. Longing filled her insides. She needed His guidance and help.

"Yoo, hoo, Ashton." Mrs. Babbage waved and made her way through the trees that bordered her property. Ashton's journey had been cut in half by Mrs. Babbage's visit.

Ashton stood. "How are you doing?"

The older woman, her silver hair in tight curls, peered at Ashton. "I thought you should know that a couple of nights ago, I took my poochies outside. You know—so they could take care of business. I glanced toward your property and saw something. Since I know James isn't staying in the guest room any longer, I think it only prudent to tell you."

Ashton frowned. "What?"

"Someone was out back—by the woods. I wouldn't think you'd be tramping out in the trees at that time of night, would you?"

Ashton rolled her eyes. "No, of course not."

"I could see a light bobbing up and down. They had some kind of small flashlight. Whoever it was ran across your yard. Then I heard an engine rumble. Not like a car but more like a motorcycle."

Ashton gripped the neck of her t-shirt and crinkled it into a wad. Mrs. Babbage had heard a motorcycle as well, but Ashton didn't want to worry her neighbor. "I'm beginning to believe that kids are breaking in on a dare or something. Trying to get to the bottom of the whole legend of the gems, James and I did an exhaustive search of the entire house. We looked everywhere for them. There are no gems. The legend is just that."

Mrs. Babbage nodded. "I'm sure that's it. If you looked the place up and down, and Gina never said anything about them, I'm sure they don't exist."

Ashton nodded. "I think these kids will stop after they grow tired of it."

As much as she wanted to believe her own words, Ashton sensed it was much more than kids. Someone was serious about finding those gems. What might they do to get them?

James lay on his back staring at the exposed timber of his bedroom. His dealings with Robert today had dredged up Robert's previous claim that Bethany had loved him, that the two may have had an affair. Digesting this information and determining if Robert told the truth would take time.

He rubbed his fingers over the Bible laying on the bed next to him. The Bible he'd neglected. "Lord, I need You. I need Your word."

He sighed, the air emanating deep within his lungs. Had Bethany and Robert...? Now that he thought of it, there had been clues. Many nights, she'd left him with the baby so she could go to ladies' card parties. Then there had been times when Robert took three-hour lunches. James had suspected nothing.

Yet, the ladies in town were not known for keeping juicy gossip to themselves. Mrs. Babbage may not have come to him, but she would've said something to Gina, and Gina would have said something, if not before Bethany's and Sammy's death, then afterward.

Mom would've heard something as well, and she wouldn't have stood for it.

If Mom had known, Dad would have intervened as well.

They were family, after all, and nothing came before family.

The thought of Bethany being with Robert piled pain on top of the ache already in his heart. Yet to be fair, he'd neglected her for weeks, thinking only of work, getting more and more involved with Pacific Cranberry. Perhaps, if she and Robert had been able to carry on a quiet affair, he had gotten what he deserved.

A sliver of moonlight filtered in through the window. Truth sank in like the beams drifting inside the bedroom—truth he'd known all along and had never allowed into his conscious mind. Truth he didn't want to admit. He'd never loved Bethany, not as a man should love a wife. He'd married her because she was beautiful and smart. A trophy wife. Dare he admit that spark had never existed between them?

He'd not understood until he met Ashton. Until she'd made him feel like a man, until his heart hammered when he looked at her. The times he wanted to put her first, and he could picture her in his future.

He flopped over in bed. How could he have messed up his life like this? Though he didn't condone Bethany's actions, he understood why she may have sought someone else—someone perhaps who looked like her husband. Since childhood, people always said he and Robert resembled twins. But they had nothing else in common.

Except Bethany.

Chapter Twenty-four

James parked his car to the side of the inn and massaged his weary eyes. After a sleepless night, he'd almost called Ashton to tell her he'd miss today. But, how could he? She might be in danger, and he had to support her.

As if Robert had wedged a knife into his muscles, the thoughts he'd mulled over last night kept him awake. Weeks ago, his cousin had hurled the past in James's face, and the guilt wounded him once again. Even if Robert lied, he'd told the truth about James and about the sham of a marriage he'd had. There was no excuse. He deserved it. The only answer now—trust in God's forgiveness. And give his heavy load to the Lord.

And stop hiding the hurt with work.

He opened the driver's door and dragged his tired limbs out of the car. Funny, how things of the heart could cause such deep pain.

He ground his teeth so hard his jaws ached as he walked nearer the inn's garden. He needed the tranquility of the trees, the shrubs, the flowers.

Nearer the deck, Ashton bent over the flowerbed, a spade in her hand.

"Hey, that's my job."

Her womanly shape, her bright green eyes, her captivating smile—she lifted part of his burden.

She rose and turned toward him. "You're right about the garden. I find peace here." Dark circles beneath her eyes told another story—she hurt, too.

Tension released from his shoulders. Ashton needed him, and he wanted to be available. "This weather is too nice to ignore." He reached for her hand. "Let's forget gardening for a moment and take a walk."

Ashton's smaller hand in his stirred him like never before. True, she made him glad he was a man, but it was more. He wanted the best for her. Dare he admit. Though the dust from the past had barely settled, he wanted to enjoy life with her, to grow old with her.

She squeezed his hand and strolled by his side down the path, around the fountain and to the northern perimeter of the inn. "The garden's fragrance reminds me of my teens when I spent time with Aunt Gina."

James stopped and faced her. "I wish there was something I could do to help with what's going on with the inn."

"You are doing what I need. Knowing you'll be here in minutes if I need you is enough."

He laced his hand through a strand of her hair. "There are times when I wish I could hold you all night, through the scary moments," he whispered. "To keep you safe." He searched her eyes for a clue of what she felt. "But not now," he laughed, "I don't want to give Mrs. Babbage any reason to spread gossip about us."

She smiled, erasing the puffy, dark circles beneath her eyes and lifted his hand to her lips.

James drew her closer, savoring her rose scent and soft skin. He sighed and tightened his hold as she slipped her arms around his neck. A whisper of the cool breeze brushed his cheek. He could be with her forever.

Something over her shoulder caught his attention, dispelling the magic moment. A few feet away, mud caked the ground. He moved from the embrace, still gripping her hand. "Over here."

Ashton turned and gazed in the direction he indicated.

They walked down the rock path several feet and stopped. Would this worry her even more? "Have you been in this part of the grounds in the last day or so?"

"No."

He bent closer to the soil. "Footprints. They aren't likely to be a woman's, either. They're bigger than mine, I think."

She looked toward the perimeter of the property where he'd parked his car. "There's something I haven't had a chance to tell you."

His stomach knotted. "What is it?"

"Mrs. Babbage saw lights in the backyard close to the woods. She said it was late and that someone ran through the yard as if trying to get away." She shivered. "Then she heard sounds like a motorcycle."

James grasped Ashton's hand. "Let's take a look."

A greenbelt bordered the north edge of the property. Peering at the ground, he drew Ashton nearer. "Look at this set of markings. Maybe they explain what you and Mrs. Babbage have been hearing."

Near a row of trees, James bent down.

An impression in the dirt which looked like a miniature railroad track extended beyond his view. He followed the markings past the western point of the inn's border. "Motorcycle tracks."

Ashton released a long breath. "Mrs. Babbage was right. She did hear a motorcycle." She gripped his arm. "And I've not only heard that same thing, I know now that the woman in town definitely had to be following me. This is serious."

Ashton thrashed, rumpling her sheet into a jumble. For the hundredth time, she ordered herself to relax and go to sleep. No luck. Her phone's clock read an hour since she'd turned off the light. In the past, slipping into la-la land hadn't been a problem.

She sat up in bed. Understanding the problem was one thing, doing something about it another. Before, each time the sounds awakened her, she hadn't been prepared—only a vulnerable, unconscious person. The truth was—falling asleep was too scary.

She straightened her sheets and snuggled under her down-filled comforter. Memories of James's arms around her quieted some of the burden. If only she could roll over in bed and reach for him. To cuddle into his protective arms.

Her cheeks warmed. The privilege of spending the night in James's embrace came only after marriage. Standards Aunt Gina had instilled in her earlier in her life. Morals she believed in.

She patted the bed. "Maxwell, come here."

He jumped on the bed then a squeak and the sound of footsteps jolted her upright and sent her pulse hammering. She clamped a hand over her mouth and reached for her gun. *Phone James.*

He must've expected her call as he answered on the second ring. "Be there in five minutes. Stay in your apartment and secure the lock."

With her ear against her apartment door, she held her breath and listened, her gun clutched in her hand. No sounds now.

In what seemed an hour, a key turned in the lock at the inn's entrance. The door creaked shut.

"It's me," James whispered.

Heart pounding, she fought tears. She laid the gun on the side table, threw open the door, and switched on the hall light.

James's wide shoulders and muscular arms invited her to come near. She rushed toward him, melting into his embrace. Later she'd regret allowing herself to relent to fear, but now she didn't care.

A faint aroma of aftershave and lemongrass soap tickled her nose. His arms were strong around her. "We'd better investigate. You said you heard footsteps on the stairs."

Ashton nodded. "I'll get my gun."

James patted his waist. "I'm carrying, too. Wait here. If anyone approaches, shoot." He chuckled. "Just not me."

"If you'll check upstairs, I'll look down here."

He peered at her. "Are you okay with that?"

She nodded. "Aunt Gina wouldn't want a wimp running the inn."

"Okay. Look for places of entry."

After twenty minutes and no signs of a break-in, Ashton listened for James.

For the second time tonight, the sounds of footsteps on the stairs washed her in dread. Then she welcomed

James's deep voice.

"Nothing upstairs. Did you find anything?"

Confusion and a sense of losing touch with reality dizzied her. Her knees no longer wanted to serve her, and she caught herself against the wall.

"Whoa." James held her to his side.

"No visible points of entry," she murmured. "Do you think I'm losing my mind?"

"Of course not. Our brains can play all kinds of tricks when we're plagued by fear or danger." He led her to the love seat in the living room and switched on the lamp. "I want to show you something I read on my phone."

Curiosity dulled her fear.

He poked at his cell. "Take a look at this." He shared his phone's screen and read to her. "'Whoever listens to Me will live securely and be undisturbed by the dread of danger.' It's from Proverbs in the Bible. When we trust the Lord with our lives, we don't have to dwell on the possibility of fearful things but rest in Him."

She traced her finger down his prickly cheek. "I miss reading my Bible, connecting with other Christians."

"It's about time we went to church. Do you want to attend this coming Sunday? We can try my old one."

"I'm ready."

"And I'm ready to kiss you."

James lowered his lips to hers. Lost in his embrace, she clung to him. She'd fallen in love with the good-looking gardener so devoted to her yard—and to a new beginning with the Lord.

Now if they could only discover who searched the

inn and why?

Chapter Twenty-five

"The evening is too glorious to stay inside. Meet me at the lighthouse." James's phone invitation washed away any dread.

"I haven't been there yet."

"Follow the road from the cranberry bogs to Cranberry Cove State Park. The trail leads to the lighthouse on a little hill. We can watch the sunset."

"It does sound wonderful. After the day I've had… What's the occasion?"

"No occasion. Just time to breathe. I'll wait for you."

Wait for her? Hope filled her chest—hope that she might have a life with him, one free of danger, one free to operate the inn as Aunt Gina had planned. A place of refuge for souls who needed quiet and the peace of the Lord.

Ashton scrubbed her teeth and brushed her hair until it shone. Tonight, she'd feel the ocean breeze in her curls.

In town, she turned at the sign to the state park. Closer to the ocean, she rolled down her window and inhaled the salt air. Was it her imagination or could she actually hear the waves rushing onto the beach and retreating?

At the end of the road, maple tree logs marked parking spots. She stepped out of her car and trekked up the trail toward the lighthouse.

Trees lined the path. A few feet up, James leaned against a Douglas fir. He held his hand out to her. "Hurry. We don't want to miss the sunset."

She ran to him, and he grasped her hand as they hiked the rest of the incline. Words didn't seem necessary.

At the top of the hill, the lighthouse shot up into the evening sky. Suddenly, life wasn't all about a mysterious perpetrator who wanted to wreak havoc. She'd turned a corner and found something deeper, more meaningful. Not something, but Someone. Someone who loved her, who died for her so she could be in a right relationship with her Maker. Someone who'd created this beauty and offered freedom. He was the true Light, and His beam shined into the darkest of any day or night.

At the top of the trail, James slipped his hand around her shoulders. "Over there. The sun is setting."

She leaned into his side and gazed over the great expanse of water. Rippling, rolling waves created horizontal patterns on the surface. Where the sky met the ocean, a glowing ball of yellow sank below the surface of the ocean. Streaks of blue, pink, and gold stretched across the sky. "It's lovely."

James tightened his hold, and they remained transfixed for what seemed like hours. Finally, he turned toward the benches at the base of the lighthouse. "I have something for us."

"What is it?"

"Follow me."

Ashton grasped his hand then inched down on the old, rock seat.

He sat next to her and reached to the side of the bench. "Since I'm pretty much a teetotaler, I'd like to toast this day with cranberry orange spritzers." He popped the top on a bottle and poured the bubbly liquid into two plastic, long-stem glasses. "To the successful future of The Inn at Cranberry Cove." He clicked his glass against hers.

The tart flavor of cranberry and orange tingled her tongue as the liquid glided down her throat. Navy blue lined the horizon with a layer of peachy salmon above.

Ashton caught her breath. "A few stars have come out of hiding. Stunning."

James tapped his glass on hers again. "To better days."

Ashton smiled as she clicked his. "Days that include the Lord."

James studied her for a moment. "Shall I pick you up for church tomorrow?"

"I can't wait." She sipped the delicious drink and absorbed the amazing view in front of her—the colorful sky, the rhythmic waves, all created by God. "Aunt Gina taught me about Jesus, and I gave my life to Him when I was a teen. I'm not sure why I wandered away. But now more than anything I see my need for Him." She brushed her hand over his.

Ashton's dreamy green eyes reinforced the truth—he wanted her for his own.

A hush settled upon them now with only a seagull's high-pitched call and the sound of the waves disturbing the silence. Sitting next to her spurred him to want more, to hold her, to show her how attractive she was.

He sipped the sparkling liquid and ran a hand through his hair. But he'd have to wait until the day he called her his wife.

"You're quiet."

"I was thinking how much you've brought to my life. Your companionship, your intelligence and independence. I admire you wanting to continue your aunt's work."

"Hmm," she snuggled against his shoulder. "I'm grateful for all you've done since I arrived."

"Before, my life was at an impasse. I couldn't find my way out of the slump. You brought me hope—assurance I can start again."

Ashton whispered. "You must've loved your wife very much."

No. That wasn't it. But he couldn't tell her the truth. Not yet. "It was a tough time." More like grueling guilt that wouldn't let up.

"Do you believe God orchestrates everything we do?"

"I believe He has a perfect plan for our lives if we will listen. Yet, He's not a tyrant who forces us to do what He wants. He'll allow us to go our own way when we insist. But in the end, His choice is always the better one—the perfect one."

"Like allowing me to go through the humiliation and rejection with my job in Denver?"

"Exactly. Maybe God used that situation to bring you to Cranberry Cove and your aunt's inn."

He shifted his knees toward her and lifted her chin. He couldn't resist any longer. His lips met hers. Their kiss was long and satisfying, but before he placed himself or Ashton in a compromising situation, he pulled away. "I respect you. I suppose we better go before I'm tempted to forget I'm a gentleman."

She ran her finger along his chin line. "Tonight was a needed break from the unknown intruder at the inn. I could use more of these occasions."

James turned on his phone's flashlight to illuminate the path to the parking lot. Halfway down, bushes rustled. Was it his imagination he saw a shadow dart through the shrubs and disappear? Were they being followed? Whatever the case, he wouldn't mention the possible danger to Ashton. She'd had enough to frighten her.

THE INN AT CRANBERRY COVE

Chapter Twenty-six

James guided Ashton up the stone steps, his hand resting on her back. The view beyond Cove Community Church made his heart pound harder. The sun cast beams of light creating sparkles dancing upon the ocean's surface as if God provided a lightshow to welcome them. He chuckled at the fanciful thought.

"The landscape is picture worthy." Ashton pulled out her cell phone and snapped a shot.

They stepped inside, and James led her down the aisle to the seat where he'd always sat alone, the third row from the front and toward the left end of the aisle. Did he dare admit he liked the spot because he could glimpse the ocean from here?

A couple of church members he'd chatted with in the past nodded then smiled. Directly across the aisle, Alicia Carter from the flower shop gave him a wave. Obviously, she approved of him bringing Ashton to church.

He turned his attention to the beautiful woman beside him and then to the worship leaders on the stage.

A chill worked down his spine when Ashton's melodic soprano sang, "Amazing Grace." The reminder he needed. The song proclaimed that God had forgotten the wrongs he'd done and didn't count them against him. As a drink of cool water when thirsty, the next words quenched his spiritual need. Though once he'd been lost, now he was found.

"Thank You, Lord." He mouthed the words so only God could hear.

Though Bethany and Sammy's deaths were tragic, ultimately, he wasn't to blame. Yes, he'd failed as a husband, but God didn't remember. He'd offered a second chance.

Later, Pastor Ethridge opened his Bible. "But God proves his own love for us in that while we were still sinners, Christ died for us."

James smiled. Just the message the Lord wanted him to hear. He was ready now—free to tell Ashton about his past.

After the service, outside on the church lawn, he smiled at her. He knew the perfect place to talk. The forested city park and nature preserve south of town.

Ashton's heart soared to the lofty Douglas fir that bordered the path. Cranberry Cove's city park had to be one of the more beautiful she'd enjoyed.

James's grin and the glow on his face hadn't faded since they stepped out of church. The pastor's message had touched him, she could be sure. As it had her.

She was convinced now, that God had forgiven her for ignoring Him since losing her job—never reading His word or fellowshipping with other believers.

James peered down at her, his blue eyes filled with sunshine. "Ashton, there's something I need to tell you. Something that's hung on like an albatross for the last months. It's about Bethany's death."

"Anything." She focused on his thoughtful blue eyes and wrinkled forehead, banishing all other distractions. She'd always suspected there were things he hadn't revealed to her. She wanted him to share his burden but reveled more in knowing he'd found the freedom to do so.

He turned toward the parking lot then to her again. "Bethany and I—"

"Hey, James." A woman with long dark hair jogged up the path toward them. Panting, she stopped a few feet away. "You out enjoying the gorgeous day?"

"Leslie, I'd like you to meet, Ashton. Ashton, Leslie works with me."

"For you, boss." Leslie smiled.

"It's a ruse," James shot back. "You carry a heavy load. Your unofficial title is an official job. We're actually equal."

This give and take was too familiar to Ashton. The actions were one of two people closer than they seemed, and Ashton was the odd-girl-out ... again. Was James trying to keep both hers and Leslie's lives in balance—one woman at each place of work?

Leslie held out her hand. "Nice to meet you. Are you new in town?"

So, James had never mentioned her or his work at the inn. She shook Leslie's hand. "I'm surprised James hasn't mentioned me. I inherited The Inn at Cranberry Cove." Ashton prayed her tone hadn't held a note of sarcasm. What was wrong? Surely, she wasn't jealous.

If Ashton were truthful, Leslie was only being nice.

Leslie nodded. "How'd you two meet?"

"I was working at the inn when Ashton's aunt was alive. I stayed on to help."

"Boss…" Leslie shook her head. "Here I thought you were going home and relaxing. Why doesn't it surprise me that you'd find more work to do?"

James slipped his finger into his collar as if to loosen the tie's hold. What was making him so nervous?

Leslie jogged in place for a second or two. "You two have a good walk." She disappeared when the path veered around a corner.

Ashton shook her head. Was there something going on with James and Leslie? How could there be? Yet suspicion nagged. Why wouldn't a woman who seemed to work so close with him know where he spent most of his time away from the office? She'd been in Leslie's position once. When people worked together, they tended to know things about each other. Had James turned to the secretary for comfort after his wife died and had now pushed the woman aside? Would he do the same to Ashton?

Chapter Twenty-seven

Ashton dragged her garbage can out onto the side of the road for Wednesday pickup. After real guests began to arrive, she'd need to contract for a dumpster.

Speaking of guests, she'd only heard from the Claxtons the one time. They hadn't returned, and their absence was beginning to concern her more than their presence had done.

The looming Douglas fir lining the street reminded her of the trees in the park last Sunday when James had begun to disclose something about Bethany and his marriage. Then Leslie showed up. If only he'd offer to tell her again. She dared not bring up the subject. Bethany's death seemed way too personal to press him.

Inside, she secured the front entrance door and conjured up a mental review of her goal for today—one more step in getting the inn ready for guests. Give the unoccupied room upstairs an extra cleaning. She could open before James cleaned the workshop and she readied it for the display of her aunt's work. Before that, she wanted to plan for an idea she'd discovered in a home and garden magazine yesterday.

If the inn was to be a place of solitude and rejuvenation, in addition to the gardens, why not provide a special location in each room. A *quiet corner*—a space near a window with a comfortable armchair. On a side table, she'd accessorize with plaques or pictures and a scripture. She'd color coordinate each room and perhaps name them with the scripture reference. The first one would be the Philippians 4:13 room for any who needed strength to face the future.

She picked up her Bible and notebook from the hall's side table then froze. Sounds like footsteps emanated from the chapel. Strange, it was daylight. If the perpetrators had entered the inn, it would be a first. They usually stole in under cover of night.

She clung to her Bible and took a few cautious steps down the hall toward the kitchen. What if it were only Maxwell? Maybe he'd roamed into that section of the inn.

With a meow, he snuggled up against her legs.

No. Her cat wasn't in the chapel. If not Maxwell, then who? Sheer curiosity spurred her on. She peeked around the double doors, held her breath, and listened. The room about half the size of the rest of the inn smelled of wood polish and musty carpet.

Maxwell darted in and yowled.

"Maxwell." She hissed. "Come here."

No sounds. She took a few hesitant steps inside. She sensed movement to her left, and a chill tingled all the way to her fingertips. When she turned, the side door to the front yard crept shut. She held her breath, tiptoed toward the exit, and twisted the knob. Locked. Could her brain be playing tricks or had she finally lost her mind?

She unlocked the door and peeked outside. The lush lawn, leafy green bushes, and beds of flowers lay before her. Nothing out of the ordinary. She stepped into the chapel again. No one stirred other than her cat who'd found a wad of paper to chase.

Sighing, she sank into the first row, the chapel reminding her of the feelings she'd experienced last Sunday at James's church. Freedom from condemnation.

She took several deep breaths trying to quiet her pounding heart then flipped her Bible open to one of the scriptures Pastor Ethridge mentioned. Isaiah 53. Evil men in Jesus's day had punished and crucified him for her sake so that she could be healed. A chill prickled her arms. No longer would she walk this earth without her Savior. In the quiet of the room, she whispered. "Thank You, God, for accepting me into Your Kingdom."

She rose and headed up the aisle. Now if she could only see the opening of her aunt's inn without any further intrusion.

James's mother had called earlier in the day and asked him to join them for a family meal. Most of the time, James used his key, but tonight he rang the doorbell. Why, he wasn't sure.

Mom, wearing a happy smile, opened the door. "Come in, son. No need to ring the bell. I'm pleased you came." She stood on tiptoes and kissed his cheek.

"I'm not so sure that a family dinner is the best thing to have tonight, Mom."

Mom frowned. "What are you talking about?"

Dad hadn't shared Robert's recent stunts with Mom. But then his father would remain quiet—anything to maintain peace. Made sense. James took a few steps through the large entry with its majestic crystal chandelier and lights sparkling off the walls.

Mom grasped his arm, bringing him to a halt. "How is Ashton?"

"Ashton? Mom, we're only friends. I helped her aunt with the grounds before she passed away. Ashton is having some problems with the inn, and I offered assistance."

"Okay, son." She tapped her finger on his chest. "But I know when someone's in love. Every time you talk about her, your face glows."

James studied the ceramic tile on the entry floor. He couldn't talk about his feelings for Ashton now. "I can manage my own love life—when I have one," he managed.

She laughed. "I know, but a mother never stops looking after her kids."

He patted her hand. "You mean well."

"Marie, ask James to come in," Dad called from the den.

James steadied himself. He'd prayed the dinner gathering would be civil, but somehow, he had his doubts. "Hey, Dad." He settled into an easy chair across from the fireplace surrounded by the gunmetal gray brick of the hearth. The coffered ceiling and the recessed lights never failed to awe him.

The doorbell rang and voices drifted in, especially

one voice that generally made him cringe. But tonight, he determined to remain amiable.

Mom escorted Robert, Terrance, and Mary into the den. "Let's sit and enjoy some wine." She peeked at Dad. "Rodney, can you see to the drinks?"

James shook his head when Dad brought him a glass. "Thanks anyway."

Robert's laugh sounded fake. "My teetotaler cousin. I'll have some of that delicious wine, Uncle Rodney."

Aunt Mary patted Robert's arm. "Now, son. To each his own."

How Robert could've had such a sweet mom was beyond James. If he were to bet, he'd predict a feud before dinner or at least during dessert. If he had his way, though, tonight would bring healing for their family.

After dinner and a delicious blueberry cobbler with whipped cream, James helped Mom take the dishes to the kitchen.

"Come on in the den, folks." Dad motioned for them to follow. "We need to have a little talk."

Coffee cups in hand, the crowd strolled into the den. Aunt Mary smiled as she settled on the couch, but Robert frowned, squirming in his chair.

James pasted a grin on his lips, determined to help Dad keep the peace, whatever they were about to discuss.

Dad nodded at his brother. "Terrance, why don't you go first. Give us your opinion about how the company's running now."

Uncle Terrance cleared his throat. "Of course, there were some small issues, but Pacific is thriving. I believe we have them in hand now. We're seeing more accounts signing on with us. We even have several clients in the northeast. Our reach is growing."

Dad nodded and looked to James. "How's marketing going, son?"

"After the near loss of three accounts due to distribution issues and the loss of providing incentive to regain their trust, I believe that Uncle Terrance is correct. Our percentages are up, and the business is moving in the right direction."

Dad nodded in agreement. "That is definitely good news. Leslie seems to be doing well in her new role."

Uncle Terrance glanced to Robert and then to James. "Yes. Very well. And that leads me to something that I believe needs to be said."

Dad leaned back in his chair.

The two older men were working in tangent, and this had been an ambush—for Robert though he was likely unaware.

James fidgeted. Robert had never taken correction well.

Robert set his coffee on the side table, sloshing the liquid onto the saucer. "I had a feeling there was a reason for this family dinner." He smiled and sat up straight.

Uncle Terrance pierced Robert with one of the looks James remembered from childhood. The look that had stopped both boys from broaching any foolishness when they were younger.

James shrank back, though he knew he'd done nothing to incur Uncle Terrance's wrath.

"And what were you expecting?" Uncle Terrance asked.

"The two of you aren't young men any longer. I've suspected for some time that you'd be stepping down."

James coughed into his hand, more out of discomfort than anything.

Robert glared at James. "What's your problem?" He frowned at Dad and Mom. "I'm sure you're not suggesting James take over the company. Dad did his time as underdog. His son should step into the role. That's only fair."

"Robert—" Dad started.

Though fury smoldered in his gut, James quelled the explosion ready to erupt. What good would it do? Robert was misreading the entire family meeting.

"Son," Uncle Terrance said, "this isn't about retirement and promotion. This is about you."

"Me?" Robert startled.

"Yes. I can't believe that you have the audacity to sit in your uncle's home and talk about fairness. Rodney and I agreed that he would hold the presidency of the company and that I'd be the chief financial officer because we each had our strengths. Imagine my horror to find that my own son's been embezzling from the company, and I didn't know about it."

"What?" Aunt Mary gasped. "Terrance, I don't understand."

"I thought we were going to keep this between us!" Robert stood. "Why are you involving Mom and Aunt Marie."

"Because we're a family business. Because you've betrayed this family."

"Uncle Terrance …" James interrupted. "I think you're scaring Aunt Mary. The embezzlement is between the family. We've corrected the issue. Robert no longer has access to finances."

"Yet, he sits here and acts as if I've played second fiddle to your father all our lives. He took advantage of my position and of his."

"Will you go to jail?" Mary turned to her son.

"I haven't done anything to go to jail!" Robert stormed. "I took a little spending money. It isn't as if I haven't earned it."

James bit his tongue. A little longer and he'd taste blood.

"Honey," Aunt Mary put her hands to her chest. "That isn't how things are done in a family business. That sounds almost—it's almost as if I'm hearing your Uncle August and Aunt Bea."

Robert crossed his arms over his chest. "So that's it. I'm out because I took a little money from the business."

"No, Robert," Dad said. "You're not out because James did you a big favor."

"Is that so?" Robert laughed. "Like he'd ever do anything for me."

"It's not just the money you've taken from the finance department," Uncle Terrance added. "It's the hours you don't work, but you collect a paycheck. It's the accounts your cousin worked hard to obtain, and you intentionally sabotaged."

"What?" Robert laughed, but now he wasn't so assured. "I haven't—"

"Don't!" Uncle Terrance stood and faced his son. "Don't add insult to injury. You know what you did. You've known you've been caught. We had a bit of this conversation in the office, but I didn't want to have this out in front of the employees. Starting tomorrow, you will arrive to work at 9:00 a.m. sharp. You will do your job, and you will do it correctly. You are on probation, son, and someone has been watching you very closely. That person will continue to do so. If you step out of line once, I will be told, and you will lose your position in the company."

Robert didn't say a word. He stormed out the door, and the rev of his car engine announced his departure.

Uncle Terrance looked at James and shook his head. "I guess we'll be on our way, too."

After Mom and Dad escorted them out the door, James turned to leave. "This is what I was trying to prevent."

"This was your uncle's idea, son," Dad confessed. "He's hoping that Robert will mature. If not, there's no way he can work for Pacific Cranberry in any capacity."

James nodded

"You know, Mary mentioned August and Bea," Mom said out of the blue. "That's not the first time I've had reason to think about them lately. And when that happens, it usually isn't a coincidence. Do you think they're pushing Robert to do these things?"

Dad slipped his arm around Mom's shoulder. "We'd all like to give Robert an excuse, but those two were run out of town a long time ago."

"It's just that … who mentioned them to me lately?" Mom pondered. She snapped her fingers. "Ashton. She said that she had a couple staying at the inn. She called them the Claxtons."

James widened his eyes. "You've got to be kidding. Oggie and Beatrice Claxton."

"Hasn't she ever mentioned them to you?" Mom

asked.

James looked to the ceiling. "That's why I've never seen them there, and she never mentioned their names, and I never thought to ask."

"If they've been here, you can bet trouble is brewing." Dad whistled.

"Well, they've been away from the inn for some time." James smiled at his mother. "I think they sensed something you sensed as well. Ashton and I have been growing closer. Our friendship has probably hampered anything they had in mind."

"If Robert's involved with them, we need to let Mary and Terrance know." Mom wrung her hands.

"No," James cautioned. "None of us have seen them. We can't prove that the Claxtons at the inn are Oggie and Beatrice, and I don't want to worry Ashton. Besides, we don't even know that they've contacted Robert either."

Oh, but he'd just bet they had.

Chapter Twenty-eight

James planted his feet on the grass and shaded his forehead as he peered at the inn's roof. He hadn't mentioned his suspicions to Ashton about the Claxtons actually being Aunt Mary's sister and brother-in-law, n'er-do-wells back as far as James could remember.

Had they actually been sneaking in and out of the house at night, scaring Ashton? If not them, someone was. That fact forced him to put the work shed on hold for a couple of weeks.

First, he wanted to check the condition of the windows. He'd know which needed replacement and which required a new screen.

He walked around to the deck and knocked.

Ashton, in a blue sweater and white jeans, opened the door.

A glow traveled from his chest to his stomach. He averted his eyes from her proportioned body.

"TGIF. Come in and share some strawberry lemonade." She held the door open.

James strolled into the kitchen. Something about her seemed different. Maybe her demeaner reflected the inner peace she exuded—her smooth forehead and lips curved up in a smile.

He breathed in the aroma of spices and tomato. "Can't say no to a cold beverage. And I came to check your windows. I've been thinking. Most likely the culprits are entering through one of them."

She frowned. "You could be right, but you believe there's more than one?"

He'd slipped. "I don't know, but some are deteriorating. I'd like to see about replacing the worst ones."

Ashton frowned. "Which will require more funds."

He nodded. "I hope I haven't missed anything. I want to check again."

She turned down the flame on her stove. "I'll go with you."

At the chapel, he paused. "What about in here? I haven't investigated this area yet."

"Oh, yes. A few days ago, I heard sounds." She motioned him in. "I sensed someone leaving by that side door." She pointed to the exit on the left. "But that was all."

"And your visitors haven't returned?" If they'd been inside the house without Ashton's knowledge, they could've used the chapel's exit to get out.

"No. And I'm getting worried about them. I expect them back any time."

He didn't want to concern her. "Did you check outside?"

"Yes. A few minutes later. Nothing but the grassy lawn and flowerbeds beyond. I didn't find footprints or any disturbances."

Then that might have been her imagination. He was glad he hadn't said anything. He sank into a rear pew and rubbed his forehead. "This mystery can't go on forever. We'll find the answers."

"What if whoever is breaking in isn't looking for the gems but something else?" she asked.

"I've thought of that but can't come to any conclusions."

She sighed and rested her head on his shoulder. "I want to attend church again. Sunday reminded me of what I'd missed all these months."

The day he'd begun to tell her about Bethany. Had God provided another chance—right here in His house? He turned toward her and gripped her hand harder. "That day, I wanted to share something."

She ran her finger over his lips. "James, is it about you and Leslie?"

He shook his head to clear his thoughts. "What? Leslie? No."

"You haven't dated her in the past, maybe in your grief."

"No," he said. "I wouldn't do that. Not after what I have to confess to you. Leslie is a co-worker. I guess it might've seemed as though we were talking in riddles when we ran in to her at the park. She's been doing extra work, but she hasn't received a promotion. She's a good worker, and I wanted her to know I appreciate all she's done. There's something else I need to tell you."

James, not if you're uncomfortable."

"Listen to me." He straightened. "I believe that if there's to be a future for us," he studied their entwined hands resting on his leg, "and I believe there will be, I need to tell you about my past. I don't want to hold anything from you, even if I have to talk about a regrettable time in my life."

She smiled. "Two people who care about each other don't need to keep secrets. You should be able to trust me with the good and the bad. We're humans: flawed and in need of God's grace. Since God grants us His pardon, we can do the same for each other."

His heart pulsed an extra beat. He hadn't heard her talk like that before. The stained-glass window depicting the lamb and the lion situated up high and behind the altar reflected the evening sunset. "I should never have married Bethany. Please understand. I'm not blaming her."

She searched his face. "It's okay. I don't know a more responsible person than you."

"We never loved each other." He took a breath.

She ran her finger down his arm. "We all make mistakes."

"But that's not the worst part. Toward the end, we avoided each other. For months I left her alone, never treated her like a wife. We never… She didn't want me, and I had no interest in her in that way." She must've caught his meaning by the way her cheeks reddened. Even in a whisper, explaining how their marriage had withered and died felt impossible.

She nodded. "There wasn't someone else?" she whispered.

Not on his part. "No." His empathic tone surprised him. "I didn't cheat on her. We offered each other an abundance of excuses, not wanting to admit the truth, but we didn't behave like normal married people."

She studied her hands in her lap. "You had no marriage at all."

James turned from her and faced the altar. Maybe this was a mistake telling her the most intimate details of his marriage.

She fanned her fingers up his arm and coaxed him to face her. "I respect you all the more for telling me."

He cleared his voice. "But that's not all."

She frowned but didn't release his gaze.

"The night before she died, we had an argument."

"You don't owe me any explanation."

"She finally spoke the truth—said our marriage was a sham, that she didn't love me anymore." He needed to tell her everything.

"Perhaps the truth needed to be spoken."

"She said she wanted out of our marriage—that she wanted me to have custody of Sammy because she never wanted to see me again." He shivered and blew out the temptation to allow her to see the threatening tears.

"Oh, James. Her words were prophetic."

He gulped and lifted his finger, knowing he needed a minute. He couldn't cry in front of Ashton. Cry like he'd done so many times after Bethany's and Sammy's deaths when he was alone.

She tightened her hold on his hand and sat as if content to wait until he was ready.

"Your aunt saw me through some tough times. She read scriptures, prayed with me, showed me how to go on."

"My dear aunt."

"That last night, I'd pushed Bethany onto the bed and stormed out of the house. Ashton, I'd never touched a woman with the intent to harm before then or since. If I had only known I would never see Sammy on this earth again—or Bethany... but like an immature kid, I left. I spent the night here." He looked to the ceiling.

"At the inn. The next day I was at work when I got word of the accident."

Ashton shook her head. "I can't imagine the pain you've suffered. I'm so, so sorry."

"After that day, the inn was the only place I found peace. That and the scriptures Gina shared and the time we spent in prayer. Then I met you. I don't deserve a second chance, but God doesn't treat us according to what we deserve but by His grace." He could no longer restrain the tear that pushed its way to his eyes. He swiped his cheeks with the back of his hand.

"Shh." Ashton drew him to her. "I love you, James Atwood, and even more now for your courage in sharing your past with me."

He relished her embrace and tightened his hold around her. How long they remained in each other's arms, he didn't know. Finally, he moved from her. "I guess if I'm going to inspect those windows, I better get started. I'll tackle the lower floor first."

After a thorough search downstairs, he answered his ringing phone.

"Son, Dad here." His deep voice rumbled over the phone. "This is last minute, but your mom wants you to come to dinner. Just the three of us. We're sorry for the unpleasant scene last time you were here."

"Sure, Dad. I'll be there."

The sound of clanging dishes drew him to the kitchen. "Ashton, nothing out of the ordinary on the first floor. I'll check the upstairs next time."

"Thank you." She dried her hands on her apron. "I can't see how anyone could get into the inn from the second floor anyway. Unless they dragged a ladder to the wall and climbed up."

He chuckled. "I don't think that would happen." Yet, the possibility was still there. He prayed the culprit wouldn't enter through one of the upstairs windows before he could get them repaired.

THE INN AT CRANBERRY COVE

Chapter Twenty-nine

Ashton adjusted her wide-brimmed sunhat and wiped the perspiration from her brow. Church yesterday encouraged her like the first time she and James attended. Church grounded her, centered her with what mattered to God. "Unless I'm sick or out of town, I don't want to miss, Lord."

She knelt at the flowerbed closest to the inn's entrance and dug another hole, secured the tulip bulb, and covered the ground with soil. Now only the daffodil and hyacinth bulbs remained to be planted. Next February, the bulbs would provide colorful flowers to welcome guests.

Guests. Why wait any longer to open the inn? If only Aunt Gina were here to offer advice. Thankfully, she had James's help. She dropped another tulip bulb into the ground and stood to secure another.

The distant sound of a car's motor grew louder until a red Corvette parked in front then a man exited.

When had James traded in his Lexus?

He waved. "Ashton." Strange. He sounded as if he had a cold. Something about him was—

Now ten feet away, he smiled.

She froze. Not James but someone who looked like him. How could that be? James didn't have a twin brother, did he?

"Yes? Who are you? You resemble someone I know."

He chuckled. "James Atwood, I'm sure. I get that all the time." He stuck out his hand. "I'm his cousin, Robert." Robert resembled James, but something was missing. Though his eyes were the same color, he didn't reflect the same kindness.

Ashton shook Robert's hand then retrieved her fingers from his cold, limp grip. "Is there something I can do for you?"

Robert rubbed his neck then offered a smile that didn't match James's. Maybe he lacked James's sincerity, she couldn't be sure.

"This is awkward, but I've heard you've been having trouble out here. Before you came, I had asked your lawyer to relay an offer to you for the inn. I never heard from him."

Ashton studied him. Yes, Mr. Bradford had mentioned something in an offhand way. He must have known she wouldn't take any amount of money for her aunt's home.

"Maybe he didn't relay the offer," Robert said.

"He mentioned something. Neither of us took it seriously. You see, this was my aunt's home. She left it to me. I wouldn't sell it."

"She operated it as an inn. I plan to turn it into a home again. This grand old place, it needs to be a home not a commercial business."

She didn't like this man at all. He was so unlike his cousin. "Excuse me. This is my home, and I want to share the beauty of the place with others. My aunt was an exceptional artist, and I plan to create a place where people can visit and connect with her art."

"It's not like she can make more. You can't make a print of stained-glass." He laughed.

She placed her hands on her hips. "But I can share what she left for me. I plan to turn her working space into a showcase for her work I have."

He leaned against the spruce tree next to him and raised his palm. He was trying too hard to act as if her decision not to sell meant nothing to him. Fury, though, burned in his eyes. "I've heard through the village grapevine that you and James have a thing going."

Ire bubbled up in Ashton's throat. "We're only friends."

"No matter. James has loved and lost before. You won't be the last." He snickered.

"That's a horrible thing to say. His wife and son died." She pointed to his car. "I'd like you to leave."

"Yes, of course. I'm sorry. I completely bungled this. If you do decide to sell, I'd appreciate your keeping me in mind."

Ashton sipped in a breath. "You'd be the last person I'd call, Mr. Atwood. I asked once. Now, I'm asking you a second time. Get off my property."

After the sound of the car's motor disappeared in the distance, she sank into the easy chair in the sitting room. What a horrible, horrible man.

James's stomach growled. He grabbed the sack

containing his peanut butter and jelly sandwich from his bottom desk drawer and paused. Through the window, the sun shone bright without a cloud in the sky. Why eat here or the break room? The city park where he and Ashton visited a couple of weeks ago beckoned. Better than being cooped up indoors.

He left the building by the employees' door in back and crossed the street, heading north.

A red Corvette pulled into the parking lot, brakes squealing.

James lifted his brow. Either Robert overslept by hours or he took a very early lunch.

James strolled past an empty grain mill and a stand of evergreens then set out on the walking path surrounding the lake. He walked a few hundred feet and dropped down onto the cement bench facing the water. He closed his eyes in prayer and then pulled the wax-paper wrapped sandwich out of the bag.

The forest's air which smelled of wet moss and the needle-covered path erased some of the concerns he had about the company. Yep, this was a good idea getting out for a while. The break rejuvenated him and offered a new perspective.

Attending church with Ashton had helped even more. The pastor's message reinforced the Christian's dependence on the Lord. So frequently, he dived right into work and made personal decisions without consulting God. No more.

After the last bite, he tossed his sack in the nearby receptacle and pulled out his phone to use its Bible app.

He pressed the icon that took him to Romans 10. A scripture Pastor had talked about last Sunday. Getting saved. The concept seemed too easy. Jesus said we needed to confess with our mouth and believe in our heart. "Thank you, Lord, for the simplicity of faith in Christ."

"Who you talking to?" Leslie, in work clothes and tennis shoes, walked at a brisk pace up the path toward him.

"Leslie, out jogging again? You must be a fan."

She dropped onto the bench next to him. "I have to confess. I saw you leaving work. I figured you might be going to the park." She huffed a few breaths. "I decided to take my lunch hour now, in case you had something that needed to be done when you returned."

"You're a little too conscientious," he teased. "Robert just showed up. Seems he's been keeping working hours. Has he given you any problems?"

"He's been the perfect gentleman." She smiled.

"No, he hasn't," a woman said.

James looked up. "Ashton. How are you?"

"Good to see you again," Leslie said.

Ashton held out her hand to Leslie. "Yes, it is."

"I saw James out here eating and stopped my walk to chat," Leslie offered.

"I had to get away from the inn for a bit," Ashton confessed. "I heard you say that James's cousin had been a perfect gentleman. He hasn't. When I saw you and James, I thought I'd tell him what happened."

James stared, remembered he hadn't stood in either lady's presence, and did so. "Have a seat," he offered both.

"No. I don't want to interrupt a private conversation," Leslie said. "Ashton, if you'll let me know when you open the inn, I'll be happy to recommend it if anyone I know is coming to town." She started off.

"Thank you." Ashton waved.

"So, you've met Robert?" James asked.

"James, I think he's involved with what's going on at the inn."

She made him sit and took the seat beside him. That Oggie and Beatrice might be working up something with Robert about Pacific Cranberry had not left James's thoughts, but the inn? What would Robert want with The Inn at Cranberry Cove?

"He stopped by a while ago. He mentioned an offer he'd relayed to Mr. Bradford before I arrived. I vaguely remember it. Mr. Bradford didn't take it seriously, I'm sure. He understood I planned to keep the inn running. Robert said he wanted it for a home."

Robert would never share his dealings with James, but James could see Robert eyeing the beautiful property. "Tell me he wasn't ugly toward you."

"He was—I don't know how to describe his attitude, but he wasn't friendly. He made some insinuations about you that I know aren't true. I know you too well. I'm glad you shared with me. I might not have …" She trailed off. "James, I came here because after thinking about it for a few minutes, I realized, your cousin frightened me."

James ran his hand through his hair. "I recently learned something, and I think I should share it with you."

"What?" Ashton leaned back.

"It's about your guests."

He hoped Ashton would trust him after he told her the truth. He spilled about Robert's aunt and uncle and how his mother may have made the connection.

Ashton remained quiet for a long moment. "But there's something we're not taking into consideration."

"What's that?" he asked.

"The woman on the motorcycle."

THE INN AT CRANBERRY COVE

Chapter Thirty

Monday morning didn't come soon enough. Though James could've called Robert—or even driven to his house Friday, he needed to cool down for a day or two. He'd kept to himself all Friday afternoon.

He cut the ignition on his car and walked inside the building, finally ready to confront his cousin peaceably.

Inside his office, Robert propped his feet on his desk and held a newspaper in his hands.

James gouged his nails into his palms and kept his voice low. "I need the truth about last week."

Robert tipped backwards and the chair almost fell over. He righted himself and planted his feet on the floor. "I arrive to work a little early, trying to catch up on the news. Can't I have a moment's peace before you start in on me?"

James used what restraint he had left not to grab Robert's shirt and shake him. "I heard about your self-introduction to Ashton Price."

Robert looked at his watch, shrugged, and busied himself by straightening his file box. "As you can see, I'm taking care of company business. I don't have time to play games with you."

James stood with fists gripped at his sides. Pounding Robert's face would be so easy. He tightened his jaw. "I know you well enough to figure out you're up to something." He grasped Robert's shoulder so he'd face him. "Stay away from her? Stay away from the inn."

"Worried I might save her from the likes of you." Robert curled his lip. "Somebody should warn her."

James huffed. "You're not about to give me a second chance, are you? Yes, I messed up once, and I've begged God to forgive me. He has."

"You need to come back down to earth." Robert slapped his desk. "This is reality. Not some Santa Claus in the sky. You hated your wife. You neglected your son. And Bethany died knowing that. No one's going to forgive you."

James back-peddled and turned to leave. Nothing he could do now but pray for his cousin. Robert certainly wouldn't listen to anything he had to say. "She isn't going to sell the inn, so stop whatever it is you're up to."

Ashton spritzed a mix of lavender and vanilla on her pillow and crawled into bed. Even the lovely aroma didn't soothe her unease. James said he suspected that her unofficial guests never had reservations at all. He wasn't sure if they were the cause of trouble at the inn. He had been more apt to believe that it had something to do with the family business. Ashton wasn't so sure.

She sighed and opened Aunt Gina's journal to one

of the last entries—a few weeks before she died.

I fear my cancer is spreading. But I'm not afraid to journey to the next world, which will be far better than this one. My Savior will be waiting.

I've learned not to waste precious hours in unforgiveness or bitterness. When we're young, we think our days will go on forever. They don't.

Though I've had a fulfilling life, I regret one thing: not pursuing Roy when we were young, before we went our separate ways. I often wonder what our children would've looked like. Would we have had a boy or a girl? Now I have only my treasured letters hidden under the stairs. The pulley system that the inn's owner installed was ingenious. And a mystery has been solved. If Ashton ever reads this diary, I hope she understands that what I left under the stairs was more valuable to me than what I found and took from that same location. She was always a treasure hunter, but I have learned something on my life's journey: what the world finds valuable cannot compare with the moments of love and laughter and connection that the Lord brings our way. My treasures on earth are the communications Roy and I shared. What I discovered, what so many have sought to discover for so long, those things can't buy happiness. Their true value is in the beauty they can make for others to see—when they aren't seeking them for monetary gain.

A chill ran down Ashton's arm. The letters. Under the stairs somewhere, and if she was reading Aunt Gina correctly, she must have discovered the gems. She read on.

If I were to give Ashton one ruby's worth of guidance, I would say don't let the love of your life get away from you. Don't allow anything to stand in the way. Go after him.

Ashton breathed in a long breath of the scented oils. "Thank you, Aunt Gina," she murmured. "That was the advice I needed."

Her aunt spoke as if she knew that Ashton and James would find each other. Had she prayed for this? Was it part of a plan she had for Ashton?

She relaxed into the soft pillow. Aunt Gina's diary had become a treasure to her. Finding the letters was important. Gina would never have wanted Mayor Fernsby to worry about his reputation. If she ever found the gems, she'd leave them where they were. Aunt Gina was right. Some things on earth—like love—were of far more value.

Ashton picked up the journal again and ran her fingers over the words *hidden under the stairs.* The letters were here at the inn.

Chapter Thirty-one

The late afternoon sun slanted through the living room window. The antique clock on the side table read five thirty. The time James usually arrived to help out at the inn. But he'd called to say he needed to do the thinking he should've done long ago.

Since she'd read the words last night, the message in Aunt Gina's journal reverberated in Ashton's head. *Don't allow anything to stand in the way. Go after him.* Wasn't that how she'd felt, what she really wanted? She loved James, and she trusted him.

Her memory returned to the evening at the lighthouse. She knew what she'd do. She slipped into the dining room and choose two plastic wine glasses from her cabinet. She located the bottle of cranberry-orange spritzer in the fridge—the one she'd purchased after that night—and tucked everything into a picnic basket. A chunk of cheese and a pack of crackers were next. She caught her breath as she left by the inn's entrance.

Hemlock Way led to the little cabin in the woods. The basket swung on her arm as she trudged down the narrow, country road. Somewhere in the trees a bird called to another who answered with a resounding chirp. Would James be as eager to talk to her?

His Lexus was parked to the side of the house. He was doing his thinking at home. She only wanted him to know that she believed in him. Then she'd leave him to himself until he was ready.

Ashton swallowed hard and climbed the stairs to the porch then knocked. Aunt Gina was right. Ashton needed to go after him.

The door squeaked open and James peered at her. "Ashton?" The smile she'd expected hadn't shown up.

She lifted the basket. "Would you care for a glass of cranberry orange spritzer?" She attempted a smile, but it faded when she glimpsed James's downturned mouth.

He stared at her for more beats than comfortable then stepped onto the porch. "I really meant what I said. I need some time to get my thoughts together. Robert may be acting badly, but his words to me—words I haven't shared with you—they have some truth to them. I need to wade through them and give them to the Lord."

She lowered the basket to the porch's wooden floor. "I understand. I only wanted to tell you that I'm here for you. I hope that once you've had some time to do what you have to do, that you'll realize how much I care."

He nodded but said nothing.

No invitation to come in. She closed her eyes against his frown and pinched lips. Sadly, she deserved it. James had asked her for time to himself, and she'd intruded.

She opened her eyes to his expression which hadn't

changed. "I need the other James with his dancing blue eyes and sweet smile."

"I don't exactly feel like smiling right now."

As if a sudden snowstorm dropped frozen flakes on her head in the middle of summer, she shivered. "I respect your needs. I understand, and I'm sorry. I should've stayed away as you'd asked. Please forgive me."

He nodded. "Yes, of course."

She paused, waiting for him to say something, anything to assure her.

"Was there anything else?" His eyes didn't reflect the change of attitude since her apology.

She shrugged. "No, I suppose not."

James stepped through the front door into his cabin. "I'll call you." He quietly shut the door in her face.

Ashton sucked in a breath and covered her mouth. He was in so much pain. Whatever his cousin had said to him had to have been horrible.

Lead weights dragged her legs as she took the stairs from the porch to the ground, each step an effort. The bag with the bottle and cheese remained on the porch. Why did she need it?

One last time, she turned to gaze at the old cabin.

The road curved, obscuring the little cabin when she turned again. Sure, she could wait for him to change his mind, but what were the chances?

The road curved one more time, and she paused to listen for the birds who called to each other before. With the death-like silence, she heard only her thudding heart. Then another sound alerted her. The crack of wood and a man's rumble. "Ashton."

She whirled around to the voice. Did James intended to return the basket? Or could she hope he'd forgiven her for her intrusion on what she knew he had to overcome: his grief?

"Wait." James held out his hand to her, no basket on his arm. "I was wallowing in self- pity before you knocked on my door. I realized how that must have made you feel." He tilted his head. "And I realized that this time, I didn't use work to push anyone away. I did it with my attitude and my words. I wasn't angry at you. Can you forgive me?"

She took a few hesitant steps toward him then walked faster. Finally, she fell into his embrace, joy rising from her chest. "There's nothing to forgive. We don't always feel like smiling or even talking to others. I don't mind going home and giving you the space, so long as I know we're okay."

"Please say you'll come back to the cabin and have a drink with me. Forgive me for being a fool. I let someone else's words take my joy away and my gratefulness for what God has most assuredly gifted me."

The cool evening breeze lifted a strand of her hair. "I'd like nothing better."

The aroma of flowers drew James nearer Ashton until his fingers settled on the tender skin of her neck.

"I can't live without you, you know," he whispered against her lips.

A bushytailed squirrel scampered from a tree and

across their path, reminding him he stood in the middle of the forest and dusk was almost upon them. He laughed and moved from her embrace then grasped her hand. "I need a glass of something sparkly and to share the view from my back porch with you."

She matched his stride. "I'm not sure what I'd have done if you hadn't followed me."

"Forgiven me, I hope. We have a lot to talk about." He grasped the basket and opened the cabin door for her. Inside, he set the container on the counter. "For one thing, my egotistic attitude."

She stood on tiptoes and kissed his cheek. "You're a man. It's in your DNA." She laughed. "But you came after me, didn't you?"

"Hey, guys aren't all that bad." He laughed, uncorked the bottle, and poured the spritzer into the glasses.

"Got a cheese knife?" She pulled the wrap off the package.

He dug in one of the kitchen drawers. "If you consider this filet knife a cheese knife, I do."

Ashton reached for the knife and arranged the gouda cheese and whole wheat crackers on the old tin plate he'd found in the back of the cabinet.

"My choice of an hors d'oeuvre platter wouldn't exactly make the cover of *Better Homes and Garden*." He pointed toward the back door. "You haven't seen my deck. Since it faces west, we can watch the sunset and catch the evening breeze."

He walked outside, set the two glasses and bottle on a side table, and held the door as Ashton carried the cheese plate and napkins.

She set the tin plate next to the glasses. "Your

garden is lovely. It stands to reason you'd have one, as proficient as you are at the inn."

"As I'm sure you've figure out, I love to work in the soil."

They settled in a two-seater wicker lawn chair, and Ashton sipped her spritzer.

James peeked at her eyes, as green as the ocean down at the cove. "Promise me. No more suspicions and no stubborn pride. We'll share everything. You won't have to be worried about me. I'm smitten with you, and you need to call me out if I try to hide my feelings with too much work."

"Agreed."

"I should've assured you sooner." He glided his hand over hers. "I love you, Ashton Price, and I hope that nothing will part us again."

Her breath hitched, and she leaned to kiss his cheek.

The breeze carried the aroma of fir trees and pine. Did Ashton's nearness accelerate his pulse?

Too soon, she rose from the seat and rested her arms on the porch railings, gazing into the distance. "Jealousy made me act like an idiot when I first met Leslie. She seems like a very nice person. She doesn't like Robert much either, does she?"

"Oh-ho, no." He laughed. Then he sobered. "Robert and I had a little talk about his visit with you." James gritted his teeth and joined her at the railing. "I'd like to bust his lip open, but I know it would be wrong. He recently pushed some buttons regarding my life with Bethany and Sammy. I have to let God handle the feelings he caused and handle Robert."

She gripped his hand. "I read in the Bible where

God tells us not to get revenge, but let Him take care of things."

"I think it's harder for guys because returning a wrong for a wrong tends to be our first reaction. One can never tell with Robert, but I think he may be grieving Bethany's loss. He cared for her, you know. Now, he's lashing out at me."

She patted his arm. "Perhaps he'll one day be open to hear how you've learned to lean upon God."

He took a breath. "I'm at a loss as to why Oggie and Beatrice have come to town. Whether it has to do with the inn or with the company, it can't be good."

Ashton frowned and rubbed her hand over his. "They haven't come back, and they aren't answering my calls. I'm going to clean out their room and store their belongings. When they return, I'll give their possessions to them. I'll have to deal with any argument over payment for reservations if they raise it."

"I can guarantee you they made that up. They aren't very good with money."

"Would they be associated with Robert?" she asked.

In the last glow of twilight, an owl's call reverberated through the trees. For a moment, James wished he possessed the bird's mythical wisdom. "I don't know."

"Let's change the subject. I have a favor to ask." Ashton blinked her lashes in a way that only women know how to do. "I read something in Aunt Gina's journal I hadn't seen before. The general location of the love letters. I know you need time to think, and this doesn't have to be anytime soon, but I'd like your help to look for them?"

Ashton walked hand in hand with James down the road toward the inn. The evening had been a delight, and James had assured that as soon as Ashton had left his doorstep before, God had gotten a hold of him and assured him that nothing James could do would not go unforgiven if James asked.

They had reached the first turn and had another before the inn would come into sight.

"Ashton. James." Mrs. Babbage hurried down the lane from her house. Her voice was a hoarse whisper, and even in the moon's glow, Ashton could sense the woman was afraid.

Ashton hurried to her side. "What is it?"

"Something's going on at the inn." The woman grasped her housecoat around her. I was letting my dogs out, and I thought I saw someone."

"Did you hear the motorcycle again?" Ashton asked.

"No." She waved a trembling hand. "I hurried toward the inn."

A loud crash hit the air. Then another.

"They went into your aunt's work shed," Mrs. Babbage cried the words. "I saw you walking to James's house earlier, and I thought I'd come and get you."

"Did you call the police?" James asked.

The crashing continued.

Mrs. Babbage nodded. "They're on their way."

James started to run, but Ashton reached out for

him. "James, we don't have any weapons."

"You stay with Mrs. Babbage," he ordered.

Mrs. Babbage clung to Ashton. "I'm frightened for him. For you. I'm scared."

Ashton had no other choice. She needed to see Mrs. Babbage safely home before she went after James. She walked with her up the lane, Mrs. Babbage babbling in fear.

By the time she got Mrs. Babbage settled, the sound of sirens and the red and blue flashing lights told her that the police had arrived. "I need to go," she told the older woman. "I'll let you know what's going on. The police may want to talk to you, but I need to know you're safe in your home. Will you wait?"

Mrs. Babbage nodded. "Go, but please let me know everything's okay."

Ashton ran through her neighbor's yard toward the inn.

"Halt! Get your hands up," a policewoman yelled and pointed a gun in Ashton's direction.

Ashton stopped, hands raised.

"She's the owner," James said from somewhere. "She was with the neighbor who made the call. We weren't at the inn when this happened."

The officer lowered her gun. "Dispatch says this isn't the first call out here. What's going on?"

"Ashton," James came toward her, "when I got here, there was someone wearing a ski mask. They were destroying the work shed and everything in it." He pointed.

Ashton took one step and then another. "Why?" she cried. "Why would anyone do this? Aunt Gina's art ... all of her art."

A policeman stopped her from entering the work shed, but Ashton could see the damage. The workshop had been broken into. Aunt Gina's shattered art work intermingled with the shed's glass, every bit of it destroyed.

"Whoever did this must have cut himself or herself. There's a fair amount of blood," the officer who stopped her from entering spoke.

"This type of crime shows a lot of anger toward the victim," the female officer added. "Miss, have you done anything to make anyone this upset with you?"

"I haven't had a problem with anyone." Ashton raised her hands and lowered them. "The other calls you mentioned, they've been minor break-ins. I suspected someone was trying to search for some legendary gemstones that don't exist."

"You said the neighbor called this in. I need to speak to her."

"Yes. She's waiting to hear that everything's okay. I'll walk with you." Ashton led the way, looking back over her shoulder.

James offered her a smile that didn't reach his eyes.

Chapter Thirty-two

A car door slammed, and Ashton jumped to her feet. She blew a strand of hair from her cheek and rushed to the kitchen. Finally, James had arrived. She held open the door for him.

He leaned down and gave her a quick kiss on the lips. "I thought today would never be over. I couldn't wait to see you."

She stood on tiptoes and kissed his rough cheek. "It's been a busy one around here. I walked through the work shed and realized there wasn't anything to salvage. I managed to hire a man and his two sons to clear away the shed and the glass. I cried for a bit, but knowing you're okay is all that matters."

He leaned his elbows on the kitchen table. "Yeah, and my blood pressure didn't spike. Robert wasn't in. Said he had some business out of town."

"Let's forget about Robert and the work shed and take our mind off of it by looking for Aunt Gina's letters." She shuffled from one side to the other. "Maybe last night was the culprit's temper tantrum over having to admit there was nothing here to find."

James shook his head. "I'd like to think so, but it

isn't likely. This has escalated to a whole new level."

"James, you're not helping." She placed her hands on her hip.

He smiled. "I'm sorry. Let me make it up to you with dinner in Oceanview tomorrow night. I know an awesome seafood restaurant."

"Sounds good. With my new clue from Aunt Gina's diary, I think we may find the letters."

He nodded. "You said something about the stairs?"

She rubbed her hands on her jeans. "In her journal, Aunt Gina left a hint: hidden under the stairs. There are two sets in the house. I've explored them both."

"I'm familiar with the stairs from the first floor to the second and then to the attic. But where's the second set?"

She pointed to the space adjacent to her built-in computer desk. "Let me show you." She opened the door, and James joined her in the narrow hall. "These steps lead to the second floor on the east side of the house but not to the attic."

"Is there a crawl space where she might've hidden them?"

"I don't think so. As far as I know, the area is sealed off and not accessible." She put her hand on James's arm. "Even if there was a crawl space, I don't think my aunt would hide something that precious to her in a dirty location."

"Okay, let's start with the main staircase off the entry. Maybe there's a spot we haven't noticed before. If we don't find anything there, we can come back and search here."

Side by side, they strolled through the living area to the entry and the main hall of the inn. The elegant set of stairs never failed to delight Ashton—the sturdy, wide steps with the extensive landing.

James rubbed his chin. "One more time. Tell me Gina's exact words."

"Only that her letters were under the stairs." Ashton touched her lips. "Oh, yes. She mentioned something else. She spoke of a pulley system. She said it was ingenious. I'm not sure what she meant."

James glided his fingers along the handrail then touched the steps' recently polished hardwood finish. "Hmm. Under the stairs. And a pulley system."

Ashton followed him to the landing under the stained-glassed window Aunt Gina had recently created and had installed. Then they moved on to the second floor. "I've been up here ten times today." She tapped her foot on the step and pointed to the closed door in the hallway. "As you know, that door opens to the attic. Could it be for the stairs on the other side of the door leading to the attic?"

After a thirty-minute search, James lifted his palms. "Nothing here. Let's check the rest of the staircase."

Ashton paused on the landing. "That window and the one in the chapel are all I have left of her work." She said, the tears gathering. "I've wanted to take a closer look at this and haven't found time."

James stepped closer and ran his finger along the bottom edge of the glass. "Look at the design with the blue and green squares that forms the perimeter. There's a yellow rose within each. Gina's favorite flower."

"The flower Roy leaves at her grave." Ashton laced her fingers together. "Notice the two intertwined knots in the middle of the window. Do you suppose they represent Roy and Aunt Gina?"

"Could be."

A chill worked its way up Ashton's arms. "Look." She pointed to the space within the two knots. "A dove flying toward a cloud. Could it represent the Holy Spirit?"

"Maybe or Gina's love for Roy which she knew would never be fulfilled before she passed on. Maybe she wanted the window to be a memorial for what they did have."

Aston studied the design. "James ..." She stepped closer, examining the exquisite colors of what, at first, appeared to be small cuts of glass that separated the different pieces on the stained-glass masterpiece. "The gems are inlaid in the stained-glass." Her breath caught as she uttered the words.

He moved beside her and stared upward. Then he smiled and looked back at her.

Ashton clasped her hands together. She could barely breathe with the discovery. She gripped the stair post's crown. The dark brown ornate piece twisted under the pressure. The stained-glass forgotten, she wiggled the post's crown again. "Look at this."

He stepped beside her and turned it with a tighter grip. "That's odd. It's loose." He slipped the cap off from the corner post.

Ashton peered into the space where the crown had sat. "There's something here. A little latch." She pulled the ring and behind her on the landing, a section of the floor popped up.

James eyes grew wide. "This is a secret compartment." He pulled the hinged door up to rest on the wall.

Ashton clutched her throat, glanced into the space, and pulled out an ornate wooden box. Tingles ran down her legs. "I believe we've found the letters."

Holding up the stair post crown, he smiled. "I thought this thing was loose. Clever." He set the cap on top and dropped the piece in place.

A chill worked down Ashton's arms. "The stained-glass window marked the spot."

James turned back and studied her aunt's work. "Ingenious, wouldn't you say?"

Ashton cradled the box in her arms and looked to the glass. "We found them together."

She didn't know whether to laugh or to cry. She started to say something, but James placed his finger against her lips. "You need to let the mayor know we've found the letters."

"And ..."

He shook his head.

She understood. They'd solved two mysteries and only a select few would ever learn the truth.

At James's usual spot in Pacific's parking lot, he blinked with the early morning sun's rays and shaded his brow.

He scanned the empty lot then did a double take. Robert's red Corvette was parked to the side of the building. Had he slept here last night? James had never known his cousin to get to

work this early.

He unlocked the door and made his way to his

office, stopping in Robert's doorway. "You're early."

Robert turned, buttoning the cuff on his long sleeve shirt. He winced. "You idiot. You scared me."

"I'm glad you're finally making an effort." James decided to forego his suspicion.

"Not all of us are the golden boy, you know." Robert smirked. "Now, leave me alone."

Sadness softened James. Robert's life had been spent always wanting what he couldn't have. Robert needed the Lord. God was the only One who could feel the void in Robert's life.

Robert stormed out of his office and down the hall to the break room. He huffed back a few minutes later.

James couldn't help it. "Leslie accomplishes a lot around here, you know. Like that coffee you thought you'd just go and grab, but it wasn't there. She makes it for us. Have you ever told her thank you?"

"It's her job."

James stopped in his own office doorway. "She does a lot for you, Robert. You really should say thank you."

"Mind your own business."

James gripped Robert's arm. There was more than his shirt sleeve over his skin.

Robert winced again and pulled away.

Okay, his cousin had never been one who liked touch, but James had a suspicion. He decided questioning his cousin would do no good. "Look man, this feud has gone on too long. We have differences, but I'd rather us operate in peace. Would you be willing to put our old disagreements aside and be friends?"

For an instant, something akin to regret flashed in Robert's eyes.

James stuck out his hand. "We share the same family. Can't we accept each other as we are?"

Robert slowly extended his fingers then his lip curled, and he jerked his grip away. "Why should I be friends with the high and mighty James Atwood? You'll only figure out another way to show your superiority." Robert turned to walk down the hall.

"No, Robert. Please… "

The slam of Robert's door was a death knell for any friendship they might've had. He should've asked about Robert's arm. He kicked himself for his moment of weakness, thinking he could resolve a lifelong hatred in a matter of minutes.

James exhaled a long sigh, releasing a small portion of his disappointment. Nothing to do now but to get to work. "Lord, please heal Robert's heart and his life."

THE INN AT CRANBERRY COVE

Chapter Thirty-three

Ashton held up her glass of spitzer.

"Cheers." James clinked Ashton's glass with his own.

On Ashton's deck, the croak of the tree frogs and the locusts' hisses reminded him that night had fallen. "Thanks for feeding me so late. The virtual stockholders meeting ran over. I'm sorry I had to cancel our dinner date."

Ashton wouldn't admit it, but she liked being alone here with James rather than in a restaurant sharing the view with the other patrons. "It's light. Fresh fruit, camembert slices and crackers, and spicy meatballs."

"Probably better than eating steak and potatoes this late." He speared a meatball.

"Yoo hoo, Ashton, you have a visitor—again." Mrs. Babbage stepped through the little opening in the bushes on the east side of the property. "This way, Mayor." She waved. "The mayor is out front again. I noticed the two of you out here, and I thought you might not hear him."

"I called him." Ashton smiled. "He didn't think he could get away early from a town council meeting, so I hadn't mentioned it. Thank you, Mrs. Babbage. Won't you join us for a light snack?"

Mrs. Babbage stopped before climbing the steps. "No, thank you, dear. I never eat after a certain time, and I don't want to leave my house too long—with all that's been going on." She backed away, almost doing a curtsy for the mayor as he stopped in front of her.

"Evening, Ethel. Nice to see you again." He held a sizeable box in his hand.

"Always good to see you," Mrs. Babbage attempted a half-smile.

"I'm going to walk her to her house," James said and followed after Mrs. Babbage.

"Mrs. Babbage has been very nervous since the destruction of the work shed," Ashton said.

The mayor made his way up the porch steps.

"Would you like to join us?" Ashton asked.

"Thank you, but I had a big dinner before the meeting. Ashton, I heard about the vandalism to your aunt's work. I don't feel it's right for me to keep this." He held out the box.

Ashton took it from him and lifted the lid. Inside, he'd placed the stained-glass Ashton had gifted him. "Oh no. This is yours." She replaced the lid and held it out to him. "That was safely in your possession, and I hope that you will continue to keep it safe."

He sat in the chair James had vacated. "I'm sorry that happened."

"Word travels fast." She managed to laugh—actually laugh at her situation. "I can't say it isn't breaking my heart. I should've brought those pieces into the inn, but I had guests and other troubles. I never got around to it."

"There isn't much crime like that in Cranberry Cove. Our criminals tend to be quieter and a little more underhanded." His words lilted in a teasing manner. "But I am thankful for this gift. I will treasure it, and someday, it will be returned to you, if you understand what I'm saying."

"I pray that isn't for a very long time, Mayor Fernsby." She stared in the direction of the area now void of the work shed and Gina's craft. She slapped her hands on the arm of her chair. "But I didn't call you here for that. Would you come inside with me?"

"I'll follow you anywhere," he teased again.

She led him through the house and to the stairs, stopping to look outside to assure that the Claxtons had not returned while she was inside. Of course, she'd kept the door locked against them, but someone had found other ways to get inside. She, like James, suspected it had been them all along. She hurried up the stairs, knocked on their room—which she had thoroughly cleaned, and placed their belongings in a downstairs closet. They weren't there. She hurried back to him.

The mayor raised a brow. "Seems a little clandestine," he teased again.

"What I am about to show you is a secret. Only you, James, and I know about it."

"Is there a ceremony to go along with The Inn at Cranberry Cove Secret Society?"

Ashton giggled. "No. The only requisite for belonging is that you be someone I trust wholeheartedly."

"Then I am proud to be a member." He smiled.

Ashton removed the post cap and pushed the lever. The stairs began to lift.

"Hmm…" The mayor stepped forward.

Aston reached inside and brought out the box of letters. "I believe these are the letters you wanted—the ones that now belong to you."

The mayor's eyes widened. "You found them."

"In her diary, Aunt Gina mentioned she'd hidden them inside the stairs that had a pulley system. James and I found it, and I kept them safe in here for you."

The mayor still held the box with the stained glass. He nearly dropped it, and Ashton juggled the box of letters, helping him to maintain control.

The mayor slid down to sit on a step. "How can I be so blessed?" he asked. "Your aunt, she blessed me in so many ways, and I let her down in so many other ways."

"Aunt Gina loved you, Mayor Fernsby. Her love for you wasn't conditioned on what you did or didn't do. She loved you unconditionally. Like Christ's love for us."

The mayor wiped his eyes.

"I have something else for the third and only member of The Inn at Cranberry Cove Secret Society."

"I don't know if I can take any more." The mayor looked up at her.

Ashton closed the stairs, took his box with the stained-glass, and sat it beside the letters on the landing. Then she waited for him to stand, guiding him up a couple of steps. She turned him toward Aunt Gina's beautiful stained-glass window and pointed. "Aunt Gina made the window, and she had it installed before her death. I believe it was left as a message for you and a reminder for me."

The mayor peered at the work, taking it in. Tears

streamed down his face.

"Aunt Gina left a message for me in her diary she knew I would read one day. I memorized a portion of it. I'd like to share it with you, if that's okay."

The mayor continued to gaze upon her aunt's craftsmanship.

"She wrote, 'what the world finds valuable cannot compare with the moments of love and laughter and connection that the Lord brings our way. My treasures on earth are the communications Roy and I shared.'"

The mayor lowered his head. "I let her down."

"She loved you, Mayor Fernsby, with all her heart. And in that message with me, she shared words that led me to something else. You'll find it in the stained-glass window."

The mayor again gazed upon the work.

"The corners of the edging. Do you see them?" Ashton leaned close to the mayor. "The gems. She's blended them in with the glass. She did it so well that someone casually glancing at the glass wouldn't realize, but once you see them, they can't be unseen," she whispered the truth close to his ears. "What she had with you was more valuable than those stones. Aunt Gina told me so."

James entered the inn and came toward them.

The Mayor's eyes widened. He turned toward Ashton, and James who stood at the foot of the stairs. He stooped down and gathered his boxes and didn't speak for some time. Then he cleared his throat. "You have blessed me beyond words. I hope, Ashton—and James—that we can be friends."

Ashton offered the mayor a sideways hug, avoiding the pointed end of the boxes. "I'd like that very much.

After all, we are The Inn at Cranberry Cove Secret Society."

"Me, too, sir," James agreed, and then turned to Ashton. "And we are what?"

The mayor laughed aloud.

"I'll tell you all about it," Ashton promised.

The mayor walked out the front door and stopped before taking the steps. "I meant what I said. This artwork and these letters will be preserved for you. They are both the legacy of a woman more gracious and loving than I ever was to her."

Chapter Thirty-four

The text from Dad read: *I need to see you in my office ASAP.* James glanced at the screen again and wedged his phone in his back pocket. Didn't sound good.

He tapped at Dad's office door and walked in. Uncle Terrance stood beside Dad's desk. "What's up?" A bit causal but he needed to stay positive.

"Sit down," Dad said.

James slid into the chair, gripping the arm rests. "That serious, huh?"

"Robert took off a day last week." Uncle Terrance shifted nervously.

"I think he's entitled to time off," James offered the olive branch.

"Yes, despite all the time he's taken without claiming it, but this time, he took time off for company business," Dad said.

"Rodney, you're being kind for my sake. James, he took off to undermine you, and in undermining you, he could have lost us one of the largest accounts we've had for years. If Oceanview Health Food Market's owner hadn't banked on our prior reputation and placed a call, we'd be scrambling." Terrance paced. "James, it's time Robert leave the company."

"Wait." James got to his feet. "Are you sure it was Robert?"

Dad nodded. "I spoke to the owner myself. He stated that Robert came in, dropped a few hints about our business, and stated that we would be charging a delivery surcharge before any future deliveries would be made. He had the audacity to ask for payment of that surcharge before he left the store."

James took a deep breath. I need to get on the phone and make sure he didn't personally approach any other accounts and take money from them."

"I have Leslie in her new office and in her new official capacity as Vice President of Distribution doing just that. Your job is to land accounts. Her job is to keep them happy with our distribution."

"And you're actually putting Robert out?" James should be happy about the removal of Robert from his daily life, but Dad had always been right. Family was much more important. Hadn't Ashton's discovery showed them what it meant to have unconditional love? He could love Robert, forgive him for what he'd done, but only a foolish company would keep someone so bent on its destruction—family or no family.

"We are," Uncle Terrance said with determination. "Your aunt is aware of it. She agrees with the understanding that if Robert ever comes to his senses and decides to work with the family, he can start in the business from the ground up."

James doubted that Robert's pride would allow that.

"When will it be done?"

"He was in his office earlier." Dad stood.

James walked with his dad and his uncle toward Robert's office. Leslie stepped out of an office that had been empty since a lower-level manager had retired. She held out her hand, five fingers splayed. "I explained to them that it had been a misunderstanding. Three of them fell for it, and I explained we would be reimbursing the amounts paid by their managers through their next order. Those managers trusted our company to note the surcharges paid as received on our next invoice. I don't believe that was going to happen." She shrugged. "I'm really sorry this happened."

Robert had been a busy boy that day. James understood his father's and uncle's changes in heart. Robert had to go.

"Not your fault. Thank you, Leslie. Good work." Uncle Terrance led the way.

James shared a look with Leslie, and he tried to offer her an encouraging smile. But he wasn't looking forward to this scene at all.

Uncle Terrance entered Robert's office without a knock.

Robert was on the phone. He jerked his head upward. "Ever heard of knock—" Robert stopped mid-sentence and stared at them.

"May we talk to you?" Dad said.

Robert shot forward, his chair nearly falling over. He coughed. "Okay." He arranged three chairs in front of his desk, and James noted he favored his left arm. "Uncle Rodney, a pleasure. You rarely visit." He uttered a nervous chuckle. "Must be a family reunion."

James didn't miss the trace of sarcasm.

Dad sat up straight. "What do you know about the

Oceanview Health Food Market account?"

Robert's face reddened. "Hmm." He clicked on his computer and scrolled to a screen with a spreadsheet. "We've made three deliveries in the last three months, sent a bill each time, and they paid like clockwork." He smiled.

Dad took his cell phone from his pocket. "So, you didn't visit them recently and explain to them that you were there to collect a surcharge before Pacific Cranberry could resume deliveries?"

Robert uttered a nervous laugh. "Why would I do that?"

"That's what I'd like to know." Dad rubbed his brow. "I could call the owner to verify the complaint he lodged. Will that be necessary? If not him, I understand there were five other customers you visited recently. Maybe they'll back you up. Maybe they'll prove the allegations made by the first."

Robert mopped his face with the back of his hand, and his gaze darted around the room.

"There's something I've been holding back," Dad continued. "When you billed our customers for deliveries never received, you committed a federal crime. They call it mail fraud. If James hadn't been on the alert for potential problems, and if Leslie had never dug into the accounts, you could be in very real trouble. The reason you aren't facing charges is because we're family."

Robert picked up a paperclip, fiddled with it, then tossed it on the desk again. His trembling chin and lips reminded James of the time Uncle Terrance scolded him for playing with his handgun.

Dad jerked his attention to Robert. "Do you want

to tell us why you would work so hard at destroying a business that has been good to you and to our family for generations?" Dad placed his phone in his pocket and folded his arms over his chest.

Robert pounded his fist on the desk. "You know what? The three of you ganging up on me isn't fair. Nothing's changed." A vein in his neck twitched. "You always gave your almighty son everything, Rodney. Was it fair he went to a better school, drove better cars, and lived in a better house?"

Uncle Terrence lifted his hand. "Now, Robert, you need to relax."

Robert's face turned scarlet, and he screamed. "I'm tired of being a second-class citizen in this family."

James frowned. "No, Robert, you've got that wrong."

Uncle Terrance straightened. "As I recall, James went to a better school because he put the time and effort into his grades and his test scores. You're driving a Corvette. James is driving a Lexus. I'm sure that your car either comes with excessive debt or you took the money from the company to pay for it. And as for a house, it isn't a better house that you wanted, Robert. You wanted James's house and everything that came with it. He recently sold the estate. You didn't put in an offer, and you didn't do that for one reason. Bethany was dead. I kept thinking you would grow out of this insane jealousy. That day I ran into you and Bethany, it didn't escape my ear that you were filling her with foolishness about James. I prayed it wouldn't create division between them. You wanted to drive a wedge between them because you wanted her."

James could feel the invisible dagger driven into

his chest by his uncle's words.

Uncle Terrance didn't seem to notice. "If Bethany hadn't have rebuked you so handedly, I would have said something, but that girl saw right through you."

"No," James whispered the word. "She didn't." He stared at his cousin. "She had reason to believe that I wasn't the man she married." He ran his hand through his hair. "Robert shouldn't have been trying to take my wife away from me, but our marriage was never a good one, and I put the walls of work up between us." He stared at Robert. "I won't let you take the blame for my marriage. Bethany and Sammy were my family, and I didn't act like it. In the same way, you have a supportive family that you've put up walls against as well. I have to live with knowing Bethany got into the accident with Sammy in the car because I'd left home the night before, and I didn't return. But you have a chance, Robert."

Robert stared at James, intense anger etching his features. "You were destined for the presidency all along." He gave a sardonic laugh. "Why wouldn't I destroy the company to keep you from a long list of things I'll never have?"

Dad bolted to his feet. "Did you not hear a thing James just said?"

As if awakening from a dream, Robert spoke. "I heard everything. His words mean nothing to me."

Uncle Terrance picked up Robert's office phone. "I need two members of security to administration. Stat."

James shook his head and frowned. Robert's intense jealousy caused him to attempt to destroy a company that so many people depended upon.

In a matter of minutes, security stepped into the

room.

"Please allow Robert Atwood five minutes to gather his belongings, take any credentials he may have, and alert security that he is no longer allowed on the premises unless escorted by security or a member of his family."

Dad led James out of Robert's office and down the hall. "Pacific Cranberry will be better off without him, but there's hope. We've discovered Robert's plan in time so that Terrance and I didn't feel that criminal charges were warranted. Dad slapped James's back. "Your idea to unofficially promote Leslie was a very good one. Without spelling it out for Robert, he had to have known he was on notice. He chose to do what he did despite that. Such is the way pride and vanity work."

Uncle Terrance joined them as they made their way into Leslie's office. "Leslie, you're welcome to take Robert's office. He should vacate it in the next few minutes."

Leslie shook her head. "Is it okay if I keep this one? I hope that one day Robert will see what he lost and will return."

"That's very nice of you, but if Robert wants to return, he'll start in the bogs and work his way up."

"I'll keep this office, just the same." Leslie offered a warm smile. "Mr. Atwood, I'm not happy that my promotion came at the demise of Robert's position. You have to know that."

Uncle Terrance returned her smile. "You saved Robert and this company a lot of grief, young lady. You earned that promotion, and you've proven to me that you deserve it. I would like you to work closer with James so that we have checks and balances."

"And both of you need to hire secretaries," Dad reminded them.

"Yes, sir," Leslie said. "And James can spend more time with his lady friend."

He was about to object and tell her she'd stepped over the line.

But Dad and Uncle Terrance laughed.

The joke at his expense, after such a traumatic time, which brought such tremendous change to the office and to the family, was worth it.

Chapter Thirty-five

Ashton followed Mrs. Mayberry, Gracie Mayberry's mother, to her car. "I can't wait for you to start working for the inn again."

Her first real guest would arrive within a few weeks, and Ashton was sure she could do a lot of the heavy work while Mrs. Mayberry gave notices to her numerous employers. How the older woman kept up so many homes was something Ashton would never understand. Mrs. Mayberry would retake her former position, and Ashton, while greeting and being available for guests would undertake the business end of things.

Mrs. Mayberry sat in her car. "You know, Ashton, your aunt had several repeat customers of her work, and those customers enjoyed collecting stained-glass work from other craftsmen, too. She mentioned once that she'd love to have people come to stay at the inn, have their collections shipped, and offer a showing of the collection of Mr. and Mrs. Somebody. She also thought about offering stained-glass artists and even painters and sculptors a venue to have showings at the inn."

"Why didn't she do that?" Ashton leaned into the

car.

"Because she said the shed wasn't secure enough."

Ashton laughed. "Well, why didn't I think of that? If I had, I may've made more of an effort to get her work inside."

"Maybe after the inn is making money again, you might think about constructing a more secure building and fulfilling your aunt's dream in that way as well."

"Mrs. Mayberry, I believe you've already showed your value to me. Thank you for meeting with me."

Mrs. Mayberry backed out of the drive, and Ashton returned to the porch.

The Claxtons hadn't returned for their belongings, which consisted of clothing and little else. She thought of sending it to the address they provided, but she and James had talked about it, and he'd assured her that their ID was probably old. They'd never lived in one place longer than six months, and they'd returned, seeing a chance to scam a new inn owner.

They were gone, and they wouldn't return.

Robert, too, had left as far as James knew. He hadn't contacted anyone. James had said his Aunt Mary was worried about him.

Ashton should feel relieved, but still, unease hung over her head like a dark cloud releasing rain on what should be happy days.

Happy days ... James had invited her to dinner tonight. She wasn't going to let anything change that.

In the entry of his parents' mansion, James opened

the box and gazed once again at the beautiful vintage ring. "Are you sure about this, Mom?" The exquisite diamonds reflected the blaze of light cast by the chandelier.

"It has three carats and belonged to my grandmother, your great grandmother." Mom rubbed a hand over her heart as she seemed to be lost in another time. "It's a family heirloom no other woman besides Grandma has worn."

James stuck the container in his pocket. Mom never spoke ill of Bethany, but she must've known there was something wrong with their relationship even before marriage. It could be that Mom held on to the ring hoping to gift it to Bethany when she could be sure that their marriage was secure, or she might've been saving it in hopes that one day she'd have a granddaughter to pass it on to. With no hesitation, though, Mom was offering this ring for Ashton.

At the door, Mom gripped both his hands. "Son, your father and I are proud of you. It won't be long before Dad retires, and you become president." She touched her lips with her index finger. "Don't tell him I said that."

His heart raced, drumming in his chest. He'd had an inkling the job was his, but Dad hadn't let on yet.

"But I want you to promise me that no matter what, you will not let your work at the office overshadow your home life if Ashton says yes." Mom averted her gaze to her feet. "I regret Robert was forced to leave the company. Dad and I are praying for him."

He squeezed her hands. "Me, too. And right now, you can pray for me. I'm proposing to Ashton this evening."

Mom's face brightened. "That's so exciting. You have our full blessings."

Warmth spread through him. "She did tell me that Mrs. Mayberry accepted her position back at the inn. That means that both of us will have no excuse to let work come between us."

"I'm so happy for you. Where are you planning to propose?"

James lifted his palm. "All I'm going to say is it's happening this evening. The night will call for my kitchen skills and something sweet."

She grinned. "You're not telling?"

"Nope. Guess I better go. I've got work to do."

Mom kissed his cheek. "Can't wait to hear about it."

James pulled out from the driveway and headed to the bakery. Ashton thought they were dining out, but the ingredients for the dinner waited in his kitchen. He only needed to pick up the cake he'd ordered. Ashton said she'd be at his house around six for appetizers, but she had no idea of the purpose.

Ashton turned on her wipers as she maneuvered her car down the forest road to James's house. He'd asked for her to drive there rather than for him to pick her up, telling her to dress up if she wished or to come casual.

She hadn't had a chance to wear her aqua silk blouse paired with the checked pencil skirt since she'd left Denver. She wobbled a little in her high heel shoes as she trekked up the old concrete walkway.

He answered before she had a chance to knock, and the heavenly aroma of something cooking made her stomach growl. "We aren't going out?"

"I hope I haven't disappointed you too much. I didn't want to scare you by saying I was cooking."

She laughed and stepped inside. "Dinner in your little cabin in the woods sounds wonderful."

"Did you bring your appetite," he'd asked. The suitcoat and tie he wore highlighted the blue of his eyes.

"Wow, you look great. I'm glad I wore my dressy outfit." She stepped into the house then grasped her throat. "You can't be serious."

Red, pink, and white paper hearts hung from the ceiling. Heart balloons were tied to the chair backs. A vase with red roses sat on his kitchen table. "James," she squealed. "It's four months until Valentine's."

He chuckled. "I thought I'd get a head start." He pulled out a chair. "Sit. We'll start with appetizers." He poured her a glass of spritzer.

She breathed in the roses' lovely sweetness. This was no ordinary dinner.

With a towel draped over his shoulder, James set two dishes on the table then made a formal bow. "Chicken salad appetizers. Enjoy." He sat next to her and said a short prayer.

Ashton munched the cooked chicken bits in a delicious peanut sauce piled on buttery crackers. "I had no idea you could cook." She blinked her eyes. "Is there an occasion?"

"After all the challenges, I decided we'd better celebrate your moving forward with the opening of the inn."

She took another bite, savoring the nutty flavor. Was that the only reason?

After they finished the appetizers, James whisked the dishes away and returned with two dinner sized plates. Salmon fillets, with lemon slices and capers sat next to a serving of fluffy mashed potatoes and green beans.

"Oh, my favorite fish meal." Ashton rubbed her stomach. "Salmon is a popular dish around here in the Northwest."

"Yep."

She dabbed her mouth with her napkin. "How did you prepare the dish?"

He pointed to the deck. "I have a grill, you know."

"James Atwood, you have totally spoiled me."

"I hope to spoil you even more in the future," he murmured.

"What?" She giggled.

He winked at her. "Save a little room for dessert."

She patted her waist. Her skirt fit a little tighter now.

After James removed the dinner plates, he set a steaming cup of coffee in front of her. "Are you ready for dessert?"

"You made that as well?"

"It's the only dish I didn't. Close your eyes."

Ashton put her hands over her eyes and heard shuffling and then a soft clunk on the table. "Don't I get a hint?"

"You'll find out in a minute. Okay, open them."

A round cake covered with white frosting and icing roses around the edge waited in front of her. Seven candles lit the pink writing on top.

"Read the words on the cake." James bounced from one foot to the other.

Ashton covered her mouth. "Oh, James." Her voice shook. "Will you marry me?"

"Ashton Price, I thought you'd never ask. There's nothing more I want in all the world." He knelt next to the table and opened a little box. Within, a beautifully cut diamond sat in an antique gold band. Dozens of diamonds surrounded a larger stone in the center.

More than anything, she wanted to marry him, but they hadn't talked about marriage before. Would she still be able to be his wife and operate the inn? Where would they live? She fixed her gaze on the diamond. "I—I"

James eyes widened. "Ashton, what is it?"

She touched his face. "Is it too soon? Are you ready for another woman in your life?"

He continued to kneel. "I'm more than ready. I love you and can't think of anyone else I want to grow old with." He clenched his jaw. "Do you have doubts?"

She couldn't allow the poor guy to remain on his knees. There'd be plenty of time to make plans. "No. I'd love to marry you."

James slid the beautiful diamond on her finger and offered his hand. He stood and lifted her to her feet. He wrapped his arms around her. "I don't know what I would've done if you hadn't said yes," he whispered. "I was worried there for a moment."

She kissed his cheek. "We have a lot to talk about, but there's one thing I know. I love you. You've helped me through hard times. You encouraged me when an intruder invaded the inn. You explored the property with me when we found the gems and Aunt Gina's letters. Best of all, you showed me the way back to the Lord." She kissed his cheek again. His woodsy scent intoxicated her. She trailed her lips along his skin until her mouth fit perfectly with his.

James cupped her face, slowly kissing her.

Breathing hard, James moved away. "Before I forget we're not married, we better eat some cake." He kissed her cheek, and he went to the kitchen and returned with dessert plates.

Soon they'd be wed, and James wouldn't have to leave her arms. But first, she had a wedding to plan and an inn to open.

Chapter Thirty-six

Ashton had insisted that she was fine to drive home alone, but James said that he'd be right behind her in his own car.

She pulled into her usual parking place in front of the inn. She stared at her hand, thinking she'd be able to see the sparkle of her engagement ring in the light from the house. For the first time, she noticed that she'd forgotten to flip on the motion sensor lights. She shrugged and got out of her car.

The inn was dark. She hadn't thought to leave a light on. Maxwell never seemed to have a problem finding his way around in the dark, so she doubted he'd be put out with her.

She stepped onto the porch and looked down the lane. James should be coming any moment, but she didn't see his headlights on the road. She unlocked her door and entered.

She flipped on the switch on the foyer wall.

The lights failed to illuminate the area.

She clicked it up and down.

Nothing.

Something moved toward the stairs. "Maxwell, is

that you?"

Everything quietened. She took two steps and stopped.

She had heard an exhale.

"Hello?"

A flashlight lit, the glow casting Oggie Claxton's face in an eerie light.

She gasped and then recovered. "How'd you get inside?"

He swung the beam, and Beatrice came into view. "We got a key made after the first night you heard us outside and locked us out," she said. "Silly of you to leave your keys laying around when you hardly make plans to go anywhere. Made it easy to take it and return it without your knowledge."

"So, it's been you."

"Sometimes."

"I know who you are." Ashton straightened.

Oggie moved the flashlight so that she could see both of them.

Beatrice held a gun pointed at Ashton's chest.

"You're related to the Atwoods. That's why you left whenever James was around," she managed. "He'd recognized you."

"We knew it was only a matter of time before it got out that we were here. This town never could keep a secret, and my dear sister contacted me asking me if I was in the area, said Marie heard from you about our stay." Beatrice snarled. "I knew you had some of the puzzle pieces."

"And the girl on the motorcycle?" Ashton had to buy time. Surely, James would see the different light and realize she was in trouble. "There's been someone on a motorcycle. She's involved in this, too, isn't she?"

"I told you." Oggie growled the words. "Frieda couldn't be trusted to do something as easy as follow her. She never told us she'd been seen."

"Don't talk like that about our daughter, Oggie. She may not have realized Ashton noticed her."

"I not only noticed her in town. You must've thought her smart enough to sneak into the inn as well."

Their widened eyes told Ashton what she needed to know. Their daughter had been anxious to get inside as well. "Trustworthiness runs in your family, I see. But just what is it that you want? You could have robbed the place blind by now."

"Yes, we could have, but we're only looking for a few gemstones, the kind that make you rich."

Ashton shook her head. "Is that why you destroyed her art?"

"That wasn't us." Oggie smirked. "Let's not get off topic here. Where are the gems?"

"You won't find them. My aunt found them, and she got her value out of them."

"That's not true, lying lady. No one in this town ever heard of her finding them," Oggie pressed.

"My aunt was very private about a lot of things."

Oggie turned to Beatrice. "What do you think?"

"I think she's lying." Beatrice snarled. "Perhaps you should convince her to tell you the truth."

James started down his porch steps. He'd made sure he'd turned off the stove and had stowed anything that could spoil outside of the refrigerator away. He didn't know how long he'd be with Ashton, as long as she'd let him stay awhile.

Soon, they'd say good night and not have to leave each other's side.

He locked his door and headed toward his car.

Someone grabbed him from behind and pushed him against his vehicle. Then the person pummeled him in the face.

He pushed against his assailant and gained some distance from the car so that he could move.

Robert staggered backward, holding his lower arm. Blood seeped through his fingers. Rage tightened his face.

Had his cousin gone insane?

"What are you doing?" James asked.

Robert's answer was to move forward again. James moved, but Robert was quicker.

James took another punch to his face, but Robert pulled back again, holding to his arm.

Enough. James had to act. He rushed Robert, tackling him to the ground.

The blood on his cousin's arm seeped from beneath a gauze bandage, but Robert's madness must be pushing him through the agony each swing must have brought. "Robert." He took deep breaths, the exertion of holding his cousin down exhausting him. "Did you get that cut from Gina Price's workshop when you destroyed it?"

Robert raged on, taking James's energy with him. Could he tire his cousin down? James had the upper hand. Robert was weakened.

James pulled back his hand and landed a right to Robert's jaw. Then another and another.

His cousin fought on.

James pulled back and his fist hit Robert hard.

"Give up." Robert spat blood on the ground. "I think your little girlfriend might need you."

Ashton? What was his cousin talking about? Robert hadn't had time to get to Ashton first—unless he'd pulled her into the woods.

With all his efforts, James took another swing and connected with Robert's already pummeled face.

Robert lay still.

James pushed away from his cousin and staggered to his car. He had to find Ashton and make sure she'd arrived home.

THE INN AT CRANBERRY COVE

Chapter Thirty-seven

Ashton stepped back as Oggie advanced. She needed James. Why wasn't he behind her?

"He ain't coming, little lady," Oggie said, as sweet as molasses straight from the jar, though as he neared, his eyes were darker than a demon's might be. "He's tied up."

"What is it you want from me?" Ashton asked again.

"I already told you. I know your aunt must've shared with you where they are. We've looked everywhere. Before you came and after you arrived. We worked our way back in here, but we think maybe your aunt has them put away somewhere. This big beautiful place. You can't operate it without something for collateral."

"You can when it's bought and paid for," Ashton said. "And when you save money for a rainy day, and that rainy day happens to come with the death of the loved one who left you the business. Aunt Gina never told me where I could find any gems. But I know she found them and put them to good use—for herself."

Nothing she'd relayed was a lie, not that she

worried about lying to people who'd take such measures. Aunt Gina didn't verbally tell her she'd found the gems. She'd hinted at it, and Ashton had discovered them. "Look, if you'll just leave, get out of town with your daughter, we'll drop this foolishness."

Beatrice held the gun higher, right at Ashton's forehead. "You know where them gems are, honey, and I'm tired of waiting."

The front door crashed in. Beatrice dropped her guard and her gun, and Oggie dropped the flashlight as a force fell against him, knocking him to the ground.

Ashton fought her way to the gun and struggled to keep Beatrice from snatching it again. Unable to grasp the weapon, Ashton kicked it against the far wall and, instead, picked up the flashlight.

James had Oggie pinned against the floor.

Ashton swung the flashlight and whacked Beatrice on the side of her head. The older woman fell backward, curses falling from her mouth.

Ashton hurried toward the gun.

"I wouldn't do that."

Ashton turned the flashlight's beam down the hall to where Robert Atwood stood, a gun in his right hand, which trembled. Blood ran down his other arm, dripping to the wooden floor. "I should've killed you, James. Instead, I had some compassion, and I let you get the better of me again. That's not going to happen now.

James lifted away from Oggie and stood in front of Ashton, his hands out. "Robert, this is insane."

Ashton gasped at James's injuries on his face and on his knuckles. He and Robert must've had quite a fight. No wonder he hadn't been behind her. Robert had attacked him.

"Ashton, I want the gemstones. I'm tired of waiting on my foolish aunt and uncle to find them."

"You've been searching, too," Beatrice screeched. She moved toward the fallen gun. "Wanted this house, you said. You'd get it you said. Something better than James would ever own, you said."

"Don't do it Aunt Beatrice," Robert warned. "I'd trust James with that gun more than I'd trust you."

"So, you're cutting us out of the deal." Oggie moaned. "I told you, Bea. Just like your sister."

James shook his head. "Listen to them, Robert. Do you hear what they're saying? Everything that's happened to them is because of what your mother and father worked hard to achieve. They can't glean anything from that hard work. I remember when we were kids. Your mother and father used to help these two out all the time. They even worked for Pacific Cranberry, but they wanted everything your mother and father had without working for it. And when they couldn't get it, their hearts filled with envy and then hatred."

"Shut up! Shut up!" Robert pointed his gun upward and fired and fired again.

Ashton screamed and ducked as bits of ceiling fell around them.

James ran forward. He held Robert's arm up, struggling to get the gun away from him.

Oggie and Beatrice ran for the door.

Ashton remembered the gun and reached down for it. She held it in the couple's direction without a word. They stopped but then inched toward the door. "I'll use it,"s he said, her voice low and steady.

"You'll shoot us and let Robert kill your boyfriend?" Oggie laughed and bolted out the door.

A whirl of sirens and the flashing blue lights indicated that help had arrived.

James continued to struggle with his cousin. Robert brought his arm down, and James pushed it to the right. Another shot rang out in the darkness, hitting glass that shattered somewhere.

"Drop the gun. Drop it." An officer entered, firearm raised.

Ashton bent down and placed her gun on the floor.

James backed away from Robert, who held the gun in his hand.

"Think about it!" The female officer who'd answered the call about the work shed held Robert in her sights. "Drop the gun," she repeated, her hand steady. "I will shoot."

Robert splayed his fingers, and the gun fell to the floor.

The female officer rushed forward along with another officer. They took Robert down quickly and handcuffed him. Then they lifted him upward.

He screamed in pain.

"Get that injury recently?" the officer asked, no sympathy in her voice. "Well, we'll make sure it gets look at before we put you in jail."

When Ashton looked outside, she found Oggie and Beatrice were already in two separate squad cars. A third awaited Robert's departure. "There's a fourth party involved," Ashton announced. She's been breaking and entering the inn. Her name is Frieda. I'm not sure if she's married or not, but she's the daughter of Oggie—"

"His real name is August Claxton. His wife is

Beatrice, and I don't know about Freida's marriage status," James said. "I'm sure they might have warrants elsewhere."

James headed away from them and down the hall. He went into a storage area, and in a few seconds, light illuminated the foyer. Of course, he would know where to find the fuse box, and if the Claxtons and Robert had been searching the home, they knew where it was as well.

The female officer took a brief statement. "I'm glad you all are okay," she said. "You need to thank your neighbor. She saw someone sneaking around the house and said she knew you were away. That's why we're here. Sir, should I charge someone with assault."

James touched his swollen lip. "Robert Atwood, the man who had the gun. He's my cousin. I think he has enough trouble."

"Atwood—as in Pacific Cranberry."

James nodded. "Yeah, that would be the family."

The officer left.

James wrapped his arms around Ashton. "You're safe. I don't care about anything else, but I'm also afraid to look."

"At what?" Ashton held to him.

"I think glass broke. Or maybe it was the ringing in my ears at the blast."

Ashton gasped, remembering what she'd forgotten in all the excitement. She ran to the stairs and looked upward.

Aunt Gina's stained-glass was still intact.

James entered the living room and came back with a smile. "I can replace a regular window, but I couldn't have replaced that." He sank to the stairs. "Ashton, I'm sorry. This is my family's fault."

Ashton knelt in front of him. "No, James. This was Robert's fault. No one made him do the things he's done. Maybe God brought him to this point because the family has always circled around each other. Robert has never had a real need that wasn't met. Perhaps now he can turn to God. Maybe this hardship will put him in a place where God can work with him.

James placed his palms on each side of her face and leaned in. He kissed her, long and hard. "I love you, Ashton Price. I'm glad you said you'd be my wife."

Chapter Thirty-eight

In the church foyer, Ashton glided her fingers over the exquisite gold heart dangling from the chain on her neck. Nothing would've pleased Aunt Gina more than to see Ashton wearing her jewelry today. In moments, life would change forever, a new life she welcomed. She still hadn't completely absorbed the truth—she'd soon become Mrs. James Atwood. Or that her world-traveler parents would be able to fly in for the wedding.

Having them at the inn for the last several days blessed her more than she'd imagined. She squeezed Mom's hand. "You were my first guests at the inn. Kind of a test run. Now, when I open, I'll be better prepared."

"It been too long since we've seen you." Mom fluffed the swirls of white organza of Ashton's dress. "The inn is perfect. Just as I remembered from the times Dad and I visited in the past."

"I've worked hard."

"Have you set a date to open?"

"Yes, a couple of weeks after James and I return from our honeymoon."

Mom brushed a strand of hair away from Ashton's

cheek. "I still can't comprehend the difficulties you've experienced since you arrived at Cranberry Cove."

"That's all in the past. I have Mrs. Mayberry there to help, and the inn is running smoothly."

Mom bit her lip. "Honey, I wish you'd told us what was going on after your arrival. Dad and I could've come."

"I know, Mom. I didn't want to alarm you."

"Well, things are going to change in the future. We're a family. We need to spend time together."

Dad shook his head. "I wish I could've been there to protect you."

Her father's sentiment sent warmth through her chest. After many years of alienation from her parents, she cherished a new beginning. "James protected me just fine, Daddy."

"Well, let's not dwell on the negative." He straightened his shoulders. "Today is your special day, and I am thrilled you asked me to walk you down the aisle."

With a pleasant smile on her lips, Mrs. Atwood strolled down the hall toward Ashton, Mr. Atwood following.

Ashton extended her hand to James's parents and smiled.

"Call us Mom and Dad." Mr. Atwood said. "If your parents don't mind."

"One can never have too many parents doting on them," Mom assured.

Mrs. Atwood touched Ashton's necklace. "Something old," she said. "Your dress is new, our home for the reception is borrowed, and here's something blue." She slipped a hankie embroidered with azure blue flowers from her purse. "I carried this at my wedding."

Careful not to muss her updo, Ashton leaned closer to give her future mother-in-law a hug. "It's a lovely tradition. Thank you. I'll hold the keepsake next to my bouquet."

Mrs. Atwood stepped a few paces backward. "Let me look at you." She sighed. "Your gown is gorgeous, and you look stunning. The bodice fashioned with lace—it flatters you. The plunging neckline is quite feminine. You take me back to the day I married James's father."

Was Mrs. Atwood thinking the same thing? Today wasn't James's first wedding, yet she sensed the sincerity in his mother's words.

At the church entrance, Mayor Roy sauntered in, glanced around the foyer, and headed her way. He laughed. "I hope I'm not going to get too emotional. I feel like my own daughter is getting married."

She blew him an air kiss. "I'm glad you came. Aunt Gina must be smiling."

His eyes glistened like she'd offered him a fortune. He squeezed her hands. "God bless you, Ashton. Gina would've been so proud of you today." His voice wobbled. "I hope you and James have a wonderful time in England on your honeymoon."

Ashton folded her hands. "Visiting the stately gardens in Europe is a dream come true—especially now. I want to get ideas for the inn's landscaping."

Mayor Roy strolled into the sanctuary.

Two ushers in gray suits and silver bow ties approached. "Mrs. Atwood and Mrs. Price. We're ready to begin." The ushers walked the moms down the aisle,

Mr. Atwood following.

Dad smiled down at her. "It's time, sweetie."

She only nodded and slipped her arm through Dad's. James, the man who would be her forever partner, waited at the front of the church handsome in his gray tux and silver cummerbund.

James tightened his bow tie and looked around the church nursery. Who was he to argue with the secretary at Cove Community Church when she said the groom's dressing room would be in the nursery?

The baby bed against the wall made James smile. A shelf with toys stood adjacent to the crib, and a rocking chair on the opposite side of the room.

He peeked around the giraffe and pony cutouts taped on the mirror and tightened his bow tie. He tried not to laugh at the plaque on the wall over the diapering table. *We may not all sleep, but we will all be changed.*

"You'll make a fine husband to Ashton. I'm happy for you both." Dad placed a silver handkerchief in James's front pocket that matched his cummerbund. "I like the idea of your building a home on the property. That way when you start a family, the children won't interrupt the guests' stays."

"Living next door to the inn will be convenient for Ashton, and she and Mrs. Babbage have grown very close. It meant a lot to Ashton that she didn't have to move far away."

"For now, the inn is plenty big for both of you—as well as the guests."

James met his father's gaze. "You and I stood in this same place seven years ago. This time I'm here for the right reason. I love Ashton. Please pray for our marriage."

A mist settled over Dad's eyes, and he slapped James's back. "You got it, son. I pray for a long and happy marriage for you both. And I hope to see some grandkids, too. Sammy," Dad touched his heart, "is always close. Never forgotten. I haven't really told you how much your mom and I miss him."

James's eyes misted. "He's in my heart as well, and we plan to give him a few siblings."

A tap on the door sent Dad to open it. "Come in, Terrance. James is about ready."

Uncle Terrance held his hand out to James and shook it with both hands. "I'm happy for you. Aunt Mary and I want to welcome Ashton into our family."

"She'd appreciate that." James wanted to ask about Robert, but his uncle and aunt had remained silent about their son.

As if Uncle Terrance had read James's mind, he frowned. "I'm afraid we haven't talked to Robert in a couple of months. He hasn't wanted us to visit him at the prison. But we're hoping that once he serves his time, he'll return to his family. His sentence was only a little over a year, just enough to send him away to prison. I think the Lord had a hand in that. If he'd remained in jail in the area, I don't think he'd grasp the severity of what he did to you and to Ashton."

James patted his uncle's shoulder. "I'll ask the Lord to show Robert he isn't alone."

"James? Ready to go?" The youth pastor stuck his head in the door. "Pastor Ethridge is waiting."

Like James's cummerbund got three sizes smaller, he tried to catch his breath. Not that he doubted his marriage to Ashton but because all eyes would be on them, the center of attention. Was he ready to experience fatherhood, again? If he dug deep inside, he could find no other answer—yes. He was ready for everything that life with the woman of his dreams would bring.

"I pronounce you man and wife."

Pastor Ethridge's voice seemed only a dream as James gazed into the eyes of the woman who'd be his for the rest of their days. The woman he'd see next to him every morning when he woke. The woman who'd walk by his side through difficulties and triumphs.

Ashton's lips formed the words: *I love you.*

"I love you, too," he whispered.

Pastor spoke again. "You may kiss your bride."

James lowered his lips to hers, and cheering echoed against the sanctuary walls. Though most of Cranberry Cove would witness their kiss, the notion no longer concerned him. His only thought centered on the woman arrayed in filmy white.

James slipped his hand in Ashton's as they strolled down the aisle to his car and the reception at Mom and Dad's. He chuckled. "I wonder if Gina had any idea her niece would marry her gardener when she hired me."

"I imagine she did." Ashton smiled.

Epilogue
One year later

Ashton perused the buffet table in the area off the living room. She gave herself a mental pat on the back. The new space with eight guest tables provided a charming dining room in comfortable elegance.

Hot scones, cranberry orange muffins, the fresh fruit plate, and carafes of coffee, tea, and hot chocolate filled the table covered with her fall tablecloth. Hungry guests could start here until she took their egg orders.

Classical music played softly over the intercom. The ambiance she'd hoped to achieve—to include the white table linens, cloth napkins, and well-polished silverware. Five couples occupied rooms now, but next month the inn would be full. She never thought guests would have to book several months in advance.

She turned to the kitchen to help Mrs. Mayberry finish food prep.

The loyal woman dished up the homemade cranberry jam into the little glass jars. "How are you feeling, Ashton?"

Ashton rubbed her hand on her extended belly. "Thankfully the morning sickness has subsided."

"Gracie said she can fill in for you after the baby's born—at least for the first several months."

"That will be wonderful. I'll need the help."

Mrs. Mayberry peeked out the window. "You can keep an eye on the inn since you're just next door."

"I'll bring our little boy over to visit, too."

"You better."

She couldn't stop smiling. James, now president of Pacific Cranberry, a brand-new home and baby on the way, and the inn brimming with guests. The journey getting here had been hard, but God had protected and guided them. "Thank you, Lord." She chuckled. "And say hello to my sweet aunt. Tell her I miss her, and everything is going well at the inn."

The End

You may enjoy these other "Secrets" books
Secrets at Rose Arbor by Gail Gaymer Martin
Secrets of Misty Hollow by Cynthia Hickey

Note from author:

I wrote this book during the time of the COVID-19 Pandemic. In my opinion, not everything has to be about the virus. Thus, in *The Inn at Cranberry Cove*, the pandemic is not addressed and isn't a part of the story.

"But he was pierced for our transgressions, he was crushed for our iniquities; the punishment that brought us peace was on him, and by his wounds we are healed." Isaiah 53:5

Writing a review

If you enjoyed *The Inn at Cranberry Cove,* please leave a review on social media including Amazon. Many readers depend upon the opinions of other readers to determine whether they want to pick up a book or not. The more reviews an author has, the more likely readers will purchase the book for themselves. These days, with the abundance of talented authors, it's difficult for a writer to get his/her books out there. Reviews are the lifeblood of an author's career. They are so appreciated.

THE INN AT CRANBERRY COVE

About the Author

June Foster is an award-winning author who began her writing career in an RV roaming around the USA with her husband, Joe. She brags about visiting a location before it becomes the setting in her next contemporary romance or romantic suspense. June's characters find themselves in precarious circumstances where only God can offer redemption and ultimately freedom. To date June has seen publication of over 20 novels and 1 devotional.

A reader says of her debut novel Flawless: June Foster is a unique author. She has a way of looking at people and seeing what's on the inside and not what's on the outside. She loves to bring characters with unique personalities and problems to the written page.

Find June Foster at junefoster.com.

Watch for Book 2 in the Cranberry Cove Series—May, 2021.

Gracie Mayberry wants to study marine science at the community college in a neighboring coastal town. But a degree takes money, and she must remain in Cranberry Cove to help her mother support her disabled father who lost both legs while serving his country and now suffers from PTSD. She leaves her job at Starbucks to work at The Inn at Cranberry Cove while the owner is on maternity leave. When the sophisticated, good looking Blake Sloan arrives at the inn, she's attracted to the guy with eyes the color of rich honey.

Seattle resident Blake Sloan takes time off from his job in his father's thriving fishing vessel company. He admits he's followed his father's dream instead of his heart's desire—to run his own business and start a non-profit to benefit wounded vets. When he meets Gracie's father, he's sure God has placed the longing within him.

But when a stalker makes terrifying midnight visits to the humble Mayberry home and threatens their lives, Blake discovers he's also a target of extortion.

Can Blake and Gracie learn who's behind the danger that threatens them? Will a small-town girl and big-city boy find a life together?

Love can conquer forces of darkness when devotion dwells deeply within two hearts.

Would you like to read more from this author? Try June's Small-Town Series set in rural Alabama where she calls home when she's not traveling in her RV.

Letting Go

When Pastor Zackary Lawrence lost his wife and unborn child, he couldn't find the motivation to effectively pastor his church in Oak Mountain, Alabama. Now, six months later, the congregation has dwindled to less than a handful, and the bank forecloses on the building. Desperate, he takes a job at the local hardware store and reluctantly moves in with his parents.

Though Ella Russell has secretly been in love with Zack since high school, her hopes were shredded when he returned from seminary with a wife. Trying to forget the only guy she's ever loved, she throws herself into her profession as a high school counselor.

Can God resurrect Zack's life and allow him to finally discover the woman he's always loved? If Ella entrusts her heart to Zack, will he shatter her hopes once more? Book one set in Oak Mountain, AL.

Prescription for Romance

Though history teacher Scott Townsend made a commitment to the Lord as a teen, he can't relinquish his bitterness toward his younger brother after he squanders their parents' money. When a beautiful, young pharmacist seeks affirmation in a way that challenges Scott's values, he must uphold his Christian upbringing. Based upon the Biblical story of the Prodigal Son, book two is set in Oak Mountain, AL

A Harvest of Blessings

Nadia Maguire's son David is the only good thing that came from her marriage. After the death of her husband, she never expects to meet handsome Jared Abrams in the cemetery where she visits her dead spouse's grave. Though she falls for the handsome bank president, his daughter hurls a wedge between them. Will her life be a harvest of blessings or a season of drought? Book three is set in Oak Mountain, AL.

The Long Way Home

David Maguire's tour of duty in Germany is over, and he's returning home to Oak Mountain, Alabama in search of a job. After a long flight from Frankfort, he shares an Uber with Dallas resident Jada Atwood.

Jada Atwood, a registered nurse midwife, is on her way to a medical conference in Queens. If only she could live up to her father's legacy at the hospital where she works, she could prove worthy of his reputation. Marriage awaits yet her fiancé has yet to offer a ring.

When the Uber driver must make a stop to pick up a passenger at a Queens shopping center, two men who robbed a nearby bank commandeer the Ford as a getaway car. But when they discover two passengers, they have to get rid of the extra baggage.

After the kidnappers murder the Uber driver, David and Jada fear for their lives. Will they find their way home or die in a Pennsylvania forest?

Manufactured by Amazon.ca
Acheson, AB

14035106R00168